IF YOU EVER WANT
TO SEE YOUR MOMMY AGAIN,
BRING ~~A~~ TEN THOUSAND.
DOLLARS IN LITTLE
BILLS TO THE PICNIC
BENCH IN CEDARWOOD
PARK.

Dear Reader,

Being single has a lot of compensations. No one bothers you to clean the clutter off the coffee table. If you feel like having cereal or—better yet!—microwave popcorn for dinner, no one bugs you about cooking a "real" meal. And there's plenty of room on the couch for you and all three cats. But sometimes dating is fun, too. You know…dinners out. *Real* dinners. Snuggling on the couch—cats optional—while watching a video and eating that microwave popcorn. But where do you go to find Mr. Let's-Go-Out? How about a class? That's right, a class like "Dating for Destiny," as taught by Sarah Dann, heroine of Diane Pershing's *Third Date's the Charm*. Romance finds Sarah, that's for sure. So where do I sign up?

Then there's our second book this month, Marie Ferrarella's *Mommy and the Policeman Next Door*. This story may feature the world's first crayoned ransom note. Of course, what would you expect when eight-year-old twins decide the perfect man for Mom is the cop next door? How better to introduce them than by a nice—fake!—kidnapping? Luckily he's been wanting an introduction to the lady for a while, so he's more than happy to take the Case of the Not-Exactly-Missing Mom.

Enjoy! And come back next month for two more terrific books about unexpectedly meeting, dating—and marrying!—Mr. Right.

Leslie Wainger
Senior Editor and Editorial Coordinator

Please address questions and book requests to:
Silhouette Reader Service
U.S.: 3010 Walden Ave., P.O. Box 1325, Buffalo, NY 14269
Canadian: P.O. Box 609, Fort Erie, Ont. L2A 5X3

MARIE FERRARELLA

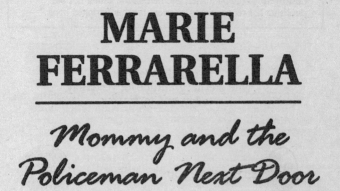

Mommy and the Policeman Next Door

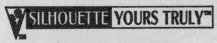

Published by Silhouette Books
America's Publisher of Contemporary Romance

To Leslie Wainger,
with eternal gratitude for yesterday,
today, and tomorrow

 SILHOUETTE BOOKS

ISBN 0-373-52049-2

MOMMY AND THE POLICEMAN NEXT DOOR

Copyright © 1997 by Marie Rydzynski-Ferrarella

Printed in U.S.A.

Dearest Reader,

Once upon a time, matches were said to be made in heaven (wouldn't it be wonderful if they actually were?), or by striking up a conversation in a singles' bar (shudder) or because Aunt Beth's second cousin twice removed has this wonderful friend who has a son who... Well, you get the picture.

These days, matching up two people who might have something in common has become far more complex than that. There are services you can go to, both on-line and off, that pair you up after you've filled out a lengthy questionnaire (and signed a lengthy check). In a lot of cases, it's become a science. The romance has been taken out of it, as has the personal touch.

I thought perhaps it might be refreshing if, rather than going through such an antiseptic process, two imaginative kids were involved. They decide to take things into their own hands and see what they can do about setting their mother up with someone they think is the perfect match—the policeman next door.

Those of you who were kind enough to pick up *The 7lb., 2oz. Valentine* might recognize the heroine's brother in this. No, that's not a mistake in typing, I did change his name to Guy rather than use Gus because, I have to admit, the former seems a little more rugged and romantic to me. For those of you who wrote to ask if "Gus" could have his own story, I hope you'll forgive the slight change and that it won't cut in to your enjoyment of the book. (Notice how I cavalierly take some things for granted!)

With all my heart, I thank you for reading.

Love,

Marie Ferrarella

Books by Marie Ferrarella

Silhouette Yours Truly
†*The 7lb., 2oz. Valentine*
Let's Get Mommy Married
Traci on the Spot
Mommy and the Policeman Next Door

Silhouette Romance
The Gift #588
Five-Alarm Affair #613
Heart to Heart #632
Mother for Hire #686
Borrowed Baby #730
Her Special Angel #744
The Undoing of Justin Starbuck #766
Man Trouble #815
The Taming of the Teen #839
Father Goose #869
Babies on His Mind #920
The Right Man #932
In Her Own Backyard #947
Her Man Friday #959
Aunt Connie's Wedding #984
‡*Caution: Baby Ahead* #1007
‡*Mother on the Wing* #1026
‡*Baby Times Two* #1037
Father in the Making #1078
The Women in Joe Sullivan's Life #1096
†*Do You Take This Child?* #1145
The Man Who Would Be Daddy #1175
Your Baby or Mine? #1216

Silhouette Special Edition
It Happened One Night #597
A Girl's Best Friend #652
Blessing in Disguise #675
Someone To Talk To #703
World's Greatest Dad #767
Family Matters #832
She Got Her Man #843
Baby in the Middle #892
Husband: Some Assembly Required #931
Brooding Angel #963
†*Baby's First Christmas* #997
Christmas Bride #1069

Silhouette Desire
†*Husband: Optional* #988

Silhouette Intimate Moments
Holding Out for a Hero #496
Heroes Great and Small #501
Christmas Every Day #538
Callaghan's Way #601
Caitlin's Guardian Angel #661
†*Happy New Year—Baby!* #686
The Amnesiac Bride #787

Silhouette Books
Silhouette Christmas Stories 1992
"The Night Santa Claus Returned"

‡*Baby's Choice*
†*The Baby of the Month Club*
*Those Sinclairs

Books by Marie Ferrarella writing as Marie Nicole

Silhouette Desire
Tried and True #112
Buyer Beware #142
Through Laughter and Tears #161
Grand Theft: Heart #182
A Woman of Integrity #197
Country Blue #224
Last Year's Hunk #274
Foxy Lady #315
Chocolate Dreams #346
No Laughing Matter #382

Silhouette Romance
Man Undercover #373
Please Stand By #394
Mine by Write #411
Getting Physical #440

1

If you ever want to see Mommy again, bring a thousand dollars in little bills to the picnic bench in Cedarwood Park.

Adam John Douglas chewed on his lower lip and held his breath as he watched the little girl who was practically his mirror image. His sister was reading the note he had written, and she was being much too quiet. Which meant that she was going to say something stuck-up when she did talk.

A.J. cringed inwardly, silently bracing himself for what he knew was coming. He'd heard it before, but he still didn't like it.

They were tackling this thing together, he and Addie, the way they always did everything, and he needed to know what she thought. Addie was better at planning things than he was. Usually. He would never tell her that, of course, not even if she tickled him and made him laugh until his sides hurt, but it was true.

A.J. rocked back and forth on the balls of his feet, feeling like his stomach wanted him to run off somewhere. He was excited about this. They were finally going to do something about the policeman next door, not just talk about him, the way they had for the past month, ever since he moved in. They were finally going to get him together with Mommy. After the policeman saw how nice she was, how far she could hit a baseball and what great cookies she could make, he'd be their daddy for sure.

Just like the daddy they had lost. He even looked like him a little, A.J. thought. At least, the uniform was the same.

All they had to do was get Mommy and the policeman to say something to each other.

A.J. had been watching a movie on Sunday about a lady who was kidnapped when the idea came to him. He knew how to get them together. Policemen always came when somebody was kidnapped.

Since then, he and Addie had been waiting for the right time to put their idea into action. It had to be when their mom was out, so the policeman wouldn't realize that they were just pretending. A.J. felt like he had been waiting forever, not just four days. He had almost given up, and then things had gone right.

Today, when Mommy left them with Summer while she went to the newspaper, Addie had seen the policeman go down to the pool. He wasn't wearing his uniform, but A.J. was pretty sure that the man was still a policeman even without it.

It was now or never.

A.J. had felt confident. Confident enough to let Addie finally see the note he had written. They would give the policeman the note, he'd look for their mommy, find her, and then they'd be together forever. It was the perfect plan.

A.J. let out a long, fidgety sigh. What was taking Addie so long? She could read faster than that. She could read faster than he could. Wasn't she always bragging about it?

"So, what do you think?"

Adelaide Douglas, born five whole minutes ahead of her brother, made the most of her seniority. She raised haughty crystal blue eyes to A.J.'s face as she shoved the note back into his hands and fisted her own on either side of her denim-clad waist.

And because A.J. hated it when she did it, she sniffed. "I think it's dumb."

A.J.'s eyes clouded with hurt and frustration. "Is not."

"Is too." Addie jabbed her finger at the paper in his hands to make her point. "Random notes aren't written in crayon."

"Ransom," A.J. corrected importantly. That was what they had called the note in the movie. He was glad he had watched it without Addie. She wasn't the only one who could know things. "And I know that. It's just a…a rough draft," he ended triumphantly.

That was what Mommy called the columns she

wrote before she handed them in to her boss at the newspaper. A.J. was proud that he remembered that. It made up for forgetting to write the note in pen. He didn't like pens. They always left black marks on his hands.

Stung, Addie grabbed the note back from her brother. "Gimme that." She read the note again, then lifted her chin. She'd found another flaw. Her fair complexion fairly glowed. "The kidnapper isn't going to call her Mommy. She's not *his* mommy, she's ours. You gotta put down 'your mommy.'"

A.J. was always open to suggestions. That was what made them such a good team. Addie loved to boss people around, and he was willing to be led. Most of the time.

"Okay." A.J. took back the note. This time, he reached for a pencil and in little lopsided letters wrote the word *your* between *see* and *Mommy*. Finished, he looked up at his sister and waited for further comments and criticisms.

Addie didn't disappoint him. "And Mommy's worth way more than a thousand dollars."

Did she think he didn't know that? "She's worth a gazillion dollars," A.J. agreed quickly. "But I can't spell *gazillion*."

Addie opened her mouth, then gave up the lie. "Me neither," she admitted mournfully, even though she hated to say so. She was older, even if it was just by a tiny bit. It was up to her to know things like that.

A.J. reached over and put his arm around his sister's shoulders. Of the two of them, he was the more sensitive one, the one his mother always said would be in demand in another seven or eight years. She said Addie was going to take some work.

"That's okay, Addie. Maybe we can say 'ten thousand.' I can spell *ten.*"

The moment of contrition over, Addie raised her chin again.

"So can I." She drew the pad over to her side of the small play table in their room and sat down. "And I've got better handwriting than you do, so I'm going to write it."

A.J. was more than happy to let his twin take over. "Okay."

With the tip of her tongue peeking out of the corner of her mouth, Addie rewrote the ransom note slowly. Her heart began to pound in her small chest as she thought of the consequences. She looked up at her brother with uncustomary uncertainty in her eyes.

"Think he'll want to help?"

There was no doubt in A.J.'s mind. "He's a policeman. It's his job." That was what Big Bird said on "Sesame Street." And Big Bird never lied. Just like Mommy.

Addie laid down her pen and studied the note she'd written. It looked pretty good, even to her scrutiny. But her stomach felt as if there was a big, wet knot in it. This was lying, and she didn't like to lie. Mommy said it wasn't right. But if they didn't do something, Mommy was going to be alone, like old Mrs. Springer. She'd have white hair and everything because she didn't have a husband living with her.

Besides, Addie really did want a daddy again. One with big arms to hug both of them with. And Mommy, too, she added as an afterthought.

She chewed her lip, just as A.J. had. "What happens when he finds out she's not missing?"

Nothing could shake A.J.'s optimistic view of the future. "He'll say he's glad she's okay."

A.J. could always make her feel better. Addie began to smile. "Think so?"

"Sure I think so," A.J. answered confidently.

"Yeah." Addie nodded her head as she pushed herself away from the table. "That's how they do it on TV."

Validated, A.J. was more than willing to render Addie her due. "Gee, Addie, you know everything."

She beamed. "Thanks. Now get me an envelope out of Mommy's room." Addie grabbed her brother's arm as he began to leave. "And don't let Summer see you."

A.J. laughed. Summer had been minding them for the past two years. She'd been fun in the beginning, playing games and telling them stories. But that was before she had gone off to the tall school. Mommy called it high school, so he knew it had to be tall.

"Summer's busy making love-y noises at her boyfriend. I could ride an ellie-fant into the living room and she wouldn't notice."

Addie was inclined to agree with him, but it didn't hurt anything to be careful. That was what Mommy always said. And when Mommy was gone, it was up to her to remember for both of them.

"Just hurry up."

Waving A.J. on his way, Addie crossed to the window. A petite eight-year-old, she raised herself up on her toes, as if that could get her a better view. From where she stood, she could just barely see the fenced-in pool. The object of their intricate planning was sitting by the side of the pool, resting. But she knew, because she and A.J. had taken to watching him, that he wouldn't be resting for long. He was always going someplace.

She looked over her shoulder. A.J. was still standing there.

"Hurry up," she whispered. "He's not going to be there all day."

A.J. didn't need any further prodding. He fairly flew out of the room before his sister could finish her sentence.

Sergeant Augustus Tripopulous, known to everyone as Guy, thanks to his younger sister's initial mangling of his name, couldn't remember the last time he'd taken a day off and actually relaxed. Probably because it had been so long ago. Even so, he felt guilty, but he put that on hold. Put the notion that there were at least a dozen things he should be tending to on hold, as well. Instead of dealing with those dozen things, he stretched out on the white plastic lounge chair and sighed.

Before him, rays from the brilliant California sun skipped along the green-blue pool water, scattering diamonds in their wake.

This was positively decadent, he thought, but he didn't care. He had this coming to him. He'd put in some really long hours in the past month.

In comparison to its larger, older and more sophisticated sisters, Bedford, California, was a relatively quiet little city. But that didn't mean that it was the Garden of Eden. Crime still reared its ugly head from time to time, like as not imported from neighboring cities that were far more developed than Bedford. Which meant far more jaded, far more dangerous. A man had to stay on his toes, even here. Especially if his chosen field was law enforcement.

Born and raised in nearby Newport Beach, Guy liked it in Bedford. He had no deep-rooted craving to play cops-and-robbers and shoot it out with bad guys. He just wanted to live in a nice place and see that it remained that way. He took it as his calling.

For the most part, he loved his work. All but the reports. And once in a while, he even got to do something significant, to make a difference. Like the time when he had found a man wandering the streets, his mind wiped clean of any memories. Guy had had nothing to go on except the engraved medallion around the man's neck. The requirements of his job had been fulfilled when he brought the man in to the local hospital to be checked out. The requirements of his conscience, however, had demanded a great deal more of him. He'd taken the man to his sister, who now ran the family restaurant. She'd put him to work and given him a place to stay. In his spare time, Guy had tried to find out who the man was.

Eventually, Guy had been instrumental in reuniting the man with his past and giving him a future that contained not only a wife, but a baby, as well. It had made Guy feel really good about himself.

And maybe, if he was being strictly honest with himself, just a little bit envious, as well.

A woman wearing a bikini the thickness of dental floss walked by. She smiled at Guy, and he nodded in response, but made no effort to follow her and take advantage of the blatant invitation she was issuing. He didn't feel like dallying. Not anymore. He'd spent ten years doing that. Now he felt like getting serious. He wanted to find someone and lay down roots.

What he wanted, he mused, was to be just like Brady Lockwood, except without the episode of amnesia. He wanted what Brady had now—a home, a wife, a family.

He had a family, Guy reminded himself. A very loving family. But in his case, that family was comprised of parents, grandparents, and a sister who thought that just because God had given her a mouth and him ears, that meant she had to talk and he had to listen. He loved them all dearly, but it just wasn't enough anymore.

Guy wanted a family of his own. A small one to start, he mused, but who knew what lay ahead? All he had to do was find the right beginning. The right woman.

All.

It was a hell of a tall order. *The* woman hadn't happened along in thirty years—what made him think she was ever going to come?

He shrugged. It was too nice a day to dwell on the negative side.

Laziness dribbled through his veins like golden honey that was slowly being poured over a stack of pancakes. Pancakes. Guy was mildly aware that he was hungry, but he was simply too tired to do something about it.

Maybe later.

His eyes began to slip shut when he felt the sudden jolt on his chair. Two jolts. One on either side of him, and almost simultaneously.

Instantly alert, his eyes flying open, Guy saw that he was buffeted on each side by a golden-headed child.

Surrounded was more like it, from the way they were clamoring for his attention. Their angelic faces were identical masks of excitement, and what Guy recognized as animated fear.

They were both yelling, one in each ear, at an identical pitch. He caught the words *help* and *kidnapped,* but little else.

Guy placed his hands on the little boy's shoulders, momentarily stilling him. "Hey, what's going on?"

Not to be outdone or ignored, Addie wrapped her hands around Guy's arm. "You've got to help us!" she cried in her best dramatic voice.

She wondered if she should pretend to faint. But if she did, then A.J. would get to do all the talking. Addie decided against fainting.

Recognition set in as Guy looked from one to the other. "You're the kids next door, aren't you?"

He'd seen them the day he moved in. Since then, he'd observed them several times as he left for work, and noticed that they would be watching him with solemn, contemplative eyes that were way too old for their young faces. He'd been in a hurry each time, and he hadn't stopped to talk. But he had promised himself that he would, very soon. It never hurt to know your neighbors, especially when those neighbors had a very good-looking mother. One with soulful blue eyes and legs that went from here to there.

"Yeah." A.J. fairly bounced up and down against him. "I'm A.J. and this is Addie. Our last name's Douglas."

Guy inclined his head solemnly. "Pleased to meet you, A. J. and Addie Douglas."

Addie didn't like to be mentioned last. She fairly shook the policeman's arm, capturing his attention. "You've got to help us."

They were agitated, there was no doubt about that. Guy couldn't decide whether that agitation was serious in the absolute sense, or in the under-ten-year-old-and-on-spring-break sense.

He cocked his head, looking from one to the other. They were almost identical, he thought. Like two halves of a golden apple. "Help you with what?"

Addie bit the inside of her lip so hard tears came to her eyes. Just as she wanted them to. "Our mommy's been kidnapped."

A.J. stared in awe at his sister. Admiration enveloped him. Addie was even better than the people in the movie.

Under normal circumstances, Guy would have said that this was just some sort of game they were playing. But the children were both so breathless, so upset, that for the moment and for the sake of argument, he decided to believe them. It was his experience that children were usually far more astute about picking up on things than they were given credit for.

He gathered the little girl into his lap. "How do you know that?" he asked seriously.

He believed them, Addie thought, her heart beginning to race. He really believed them. This was great. She wanted to squeeze her brother, but didn't dare.

"Because we saw the note. The ransom note." She said the word very slowly, afraid of getting it wrong and spoiling everything. Addie's lower lip quivered. "You can get her back, can't you? You're a policeman. I saw your uniform."

Then this was on the level, Guy thought. His heart went out to the two children. Striving to calm her, he ran his hand over the girl's hair. Poor kid. "Yes, I'm a policeman."

Not to be left out, A.J. chimed in. "You won't let anything happen to her, will you? She's all we've got. Our daddy went away a long time ago and he's not coming back." A.J. wondered how Addie could cry like that. He thought of the saddest thing he could and felt his eyes sting a little, but no tears came. "Mommy said he can't."

Guy wondered if "can't" translated into "won't." Was the long-legged woman who lived next door to him a widow, or a divorcée with a restraining order against her ex? He hadn't noticed any man coming or going from the apartment, but then, he hadn't been around all that much. The stakeout had taken up most of his time since he moved in. Some of his things were still in boxes, and he absolutely abhorred clutter.

"Would you know who would want to hurt your mommy?" he asked A.J. gently.

A.J. shook his head. Moving Addie aside, he climbed onto the policeman's lap. It was a nice, warm place to be. He vaguely remembered a bigger, softer lap. A lap that had made him feel safe. But he knew he hadn't sat in that lap in a long, long time. Mommy's lap was nice, but it was small. There really wasn't enough room for both him and Addie on it anymore.

"No. Everybody likes Mommy." He knew he should be saying something more. Something to make the policeman feel sorry for them. "You won't let anything happen to her, will you, Mr. Policeman?"

"Guy," Guy told them, trying to guess what they had to be going through right now. "My name is Guy, and no, I won't let anything happen to her." The first place to start, he thought, was in the woman's apartment. Because he didn't want to upset them any more than they already were, Guy tried to make his questions seem more like a conversation. "How long has she been gone?"

"A long time," Addie told him solemnly, nodding her head for emphasis.

"Since this morning," A.J. announced.

Addie glared at A.J. for contradicting her. He was going to ruin everything. She should have told him to stay home.

"It feels like a long time," she explained.

"I'm sure it does," Guy agreed soothingly. Very

gently, he moved each child off the chair and then rose himself. "Does she leave you alone often?"

Maybe this was all a misunderstanding. Maybe the woman had just gone off and they just thought she'd been kidnapped. If that was the case, he was going to give her a stern warning about the criminal ramifications of leaving young children home alone.

"Oh, no," A.J. protested. "We're not alone. Summer's with us."

"Summer," Guy repeated. If someone was with them, why hadn't they reported the kidnapping?

"Our baby-sitter," A.J. elaborated, despite the glaring look Addie was giving him. He could never please Addie, he thought glumly. There was always something wrong.

She had to keep A.J. from talking, or he was going to spoil everything. They had to get Guy to their apartment before Mommy got back.

"Young people-sitter," Addie corrected.

This one was going to run for office, Guy thought. He was beginning to rethink the gravity of the situation. Maybe this was a game after all. "So, can I see the note?" He held his hand out.

The plan was back on track. Addie nodded her head. "Sure," she said, with the confidence of one whose heart was pure and whose intentions were noble. She linked her small hand with Guy's and began to tug him in the right direction. "But you gotta come with us to our apartment."

His suspicions were definitely aroused. He usually

had a sixth sense about things when it came to trouble, and so far, it hadn't kicked in.

"And why is that?" he asked Addie.

Addie continued tugging. She glanced toward her brother expectantly. A.J. took Guy's other hand and pulled.

"Because that's where the note is, Guy." Addie tossed her golden head in the direction of the garden apartments. "We didn't want anything happening to it when we came down here looking for you."

"You came looking for me." So they hadn't just happened on him as the first available adult they spied.

"'Course," A.J. said with feeling. "You're the cop next door."

"Policeman," Addie corrected. She shook her head dismissively at her brother, then turned her face up toward Guy. "Children. You have to watch them every minute."

Guy had trouble hiding the smile that was beginning to bloom. "So they tell me."

Addie's light brows almost touched as a thought suddenly occurred to her. "You don't have any of your own, do you? Children?" she pressed, when he didn't answer her immediately.

Addie knew that Joey Kennedy's daddy didn't live with them anymore, but he was still their daddy. She didn't want to take away anyone's daddy. She just wanted one of her own. It had been so long since she had one.

She was beginning to sound like one of the women his grandmother socialized with, Guy thought. Always quizzing him about his life and whether or not he had gotten married since they saw him last. "No, I don't. I'm not married."

Addie nodded her head. "We know that. But were you ever married?" They were almost at the apartment, and she turned toward him, waiting for his answer before continuing on.

"No. Why?"

She let out a sigh of relief. She hadn't messed up. He was the right one for Mommy. "Just wanted to know." Addie turned again, motioning him on. "It's this way."

"Yes, I know." He followed her. The boy was directly behind him, as if prepared to block the way if he changed his mind about coming with them. "I live next door."

"How come you're a cop?" A.J. wanted to know. "Um, I mean a policeman."

Guy stopped just short of the door, wondering what this was all about. He was fairly convinced, tears or no tears, that the woman next door was not a kidnap victim, but the center of an elaborate juvenile plot.

"I like helping people."

A.J.'s eyes were wide, and incredibly blue. "Like you're going to help us find our mommy?"

There had to be a gentle way to ease out of this. "About that—"

"Here we are," Addie announced, throwing open the front door. She clamped her hands down around his wrist again, in case he decided to leave. "The note's in the kitchen."

Maybe there wasn't a way to ease out of this just yet. Curiosity urged him on a little farther. As he allowed himself to be drawn into the apartment, Guy saw a slender blond-haired girl in the living room. She was comfortably propped up against the myriad of pillows on the sofa. There was a telephone attached to her ear. From the angle she assumed on the sofa, the receiver appeared to be hermetically sealed. She was completely oblivious of the fact that her charges had left the apartment and then returned with a stranger in tow.

"Summer?" he guessed, directing the name and the question toward Addie.

The disdainful look on the little girl's face was not lost on him.

"Summer," she confirmed. Without sparing the teenager another look, Addie continued leading Guy into the kitchen. He was pretty manageable for an adult, she thought, pleased that it was going so well.

Once in the kitchen, Addie produced the envelope

with the note inside it. She handed it to him with a small flourish.

"Here it is," she announced. "The ransom note."

If Guy still had any lingering doubts that this was a game, they were quickly dispelled as soon as he took the note out and read the childish scrawl.

It was a game, he thought, and they needed an adult to play with them. The teenager in the other room was obviously unsatisfactory or unwilling. Maybe both. In either case, she wasn't part of it.

He had nothing pressing for the day, and suddenly, sitting at poolside, deepening his already dark complexion, didn't have much allure. Neither did unpacking the boxes that were still stacked up in his bedroom. Guy decided to play along.

Pretending to read and then reread the note, he finally placed it on the table and nodded, pulling his features into a grave expression.

"It looks serious, kids. I'm going to have to get right on this."

The glee that passed between the twins was almost audible and definitely visible.

Addie was almost ready to hug herself. "Then you'll help?"

"It's my sworn duty," Guy informed her. "As a policeman."

Just like on "Sesame Street." "See, I knew he would," A.J. crowed to his sister.

Addie didn't want Guy to think that she didn't have any faith in him.

"So did I," she chimed in with feeling. She looked like a little goat, about to butt heads with another goat as she lowered her head. "He was my idea."

Realizing what she had just said, Addie clamped both hands over her mouth, her eyes darting fearfully toward Guy's face.

"It was your idea to ask me for help?" Guy supplied innocently.

Addie sighed, relieved, as she slid her hands away from her mouth. It was still okay. "Yeah."

"Good thinking," Guy confirmed. "This is obviously the work of a criminal mastermind."

Pleasure flitted through A.J.'s chest. He stood on his toes, looking around Guy's well-muscled forearm at the note, as if he had never seen it before. "You think?"

It was getting more and more difficult not to smile. "I know."

Guy had always had an affinity for children. Right now, he was thoroughly enjoying himself. So much so that he didn't hear the front door opening and then closing again. Nor did he see the perplexed woman approaching.

But Nancy Douglas certainly saw him. All of him. And wondered why there was a seminude man standing in her kitchen, talking to her children.

2

"What's going on here?" Nancy's question startled all three people in her kitchen.

Addie and A.J. looked at each other, panic generated by a lack of a contingency plan telegraphing itself between them.

Mommy was home too soon, Addie thought, quickly glancing at Guy. This would spoil everything.

Led by instincts she was far too young to understand, Addie threw herself at her mother, wrapping her arms around Nancy Douglas's hips.

A.J. was quick to follow his sister's lead, although he wasn't really sure why they were hanging on to Mommy like this.

Addie turned her face up to her mother, summoning her most innocent, most grateful look. "Mommy, you're here! You're back!"

Something really strange was going on here. Nancy let her briefcase slip from her fingers as she circled an arm around each child.

"Of course I'm back." Her words were directed

at her children, but her gaze was on the man standing in her kitchen. Who *was* he and why was he here? And why was he wearing a bathing suit? "I always come back."

The fleeting glance he had had of her hadn't begun to do her justice. The lady was a knockout close-up. "Very brave of you."

"Brave of me?" Was that some kind of crack about her kids? Granted, they were a little livelier than she'd like at times, but lively was better than inert couch potatoes. She tried to extricate herself, and discovered that the twins' grasp was tighter than she'd thought. Just what was going on here? "Listen, Mr.—"

Guy acted as if she hadn't begun to say anything. For the twins' sake, and perhaps for his own amusement, he continued with the little one-act play they had pulled him into.

"Yes, brave of you to escape from your kidnappers like that," he concluded.

The death grip on her hips slackened suddenly as the cat came bounding out of the proverbial bag.

She looked down at Addie and A.J. What were they up to? And just how had they managed to involve this stranger in their game? They knew how she felt about their talking to strangers.

"Kidnappers?" she echoed incredulously.

"Yes." Guy winked at her broadly over Addie's and A.J.'s heads. He talked fast, filling her in on the scenario before she could say anything further. He hadn't been raised with Demi for nothing, he thought. "Addie and A.J. came to me with the ransom note." Picking it up from the kitchen table, he handed her the piece of paper. "They were really worried, but they kept their heads and acted just the way you would have wanted them to in an emergency." He smiled at each of the children.

That had to be the sexiest wink she'd ever been on the receiving end of. Like an independent entity, it seemed to undulate its way straight into her nerve centers. Nancy deliberately lowered her eyes to the note and read, ignoring the slight quiver in her stomach. Was this a joke someone had put them up to? And how did he figure into this?

At a loss, Nancy folded the note in half. "Emergency?" she echoed. "I don't know about that."

He didn't want her angry at them, or at him, Guy suddenly decided. With the charm that his mother claimed had been generations in the making, he smiled at Addie and A.J.'s mother engagingly. "Oh, trust me, most seven—"

"Eight," Addie corrected quickly. She didn't want him thinking she was a baby.

"Eight," Guy repeated, without missing a beat.

"And a half." A.J., afraid of being overlooked, felt it his duty to point out how really close he and his sister were to nine.

"And-a-half-year-olds," Guy allowed easily, "wouldn't have known what to do, but they did." His grin was infectious as he shared it with the children. Their mother, he noted, was going to take a little more work. "They came straight to me with the note."

This wasn't good. Addie and A.J. had been warned time and again about talking to strangers. Turning her ire on this underdressed man, she asked pointedly, "And you are?"

Addie jumped in before her mother could say anything further to make the policeman leave. "You know, Mommy, the policeman next door."

The policeman—? Looking again, she realized that Addie was right. She'd caught a glimpse of him hurrying to his car at the beginning of the week, and come away with an impression of dark, curly hair and very broad shoulders. He certainly fit that description.

Feeling just the slightest bit chagrined, Nancy fidgeted with the note. "Oh, right, sorry, I didn't recognize you without your clothes on."

A.J. covered his mouth to stifle a fit of giggles. "He's got clothes on, Mommy."

Not much, from where she was standing, and the fact was making her somewhat uncomfortable, in a curled-toes, fidgety sort of way. The few times she had seen him since he moved in, his uniform had hinted of the broad, hard physique it was covering, but this was literally shouting it at her. She hadn't given the man next door much thought, really, other than the usual bittersweet sting she experienced whenever she saw a police uniform in close proximity.

It reminded her of Tom and of what they would never have a chance to experience. She tried not to think about that most of the time.

"Yes, he's got clothes on. Just barely," she felt compelled to murmur. She was rewarded with an unsettling grin that seemed bound to follow the path initiated by his wink. Enough of this, she had work to do. "Officer—"

"Tripopulous," Guy said as he put his hand out toward her.

From the look on the children's faces, Guy realized that he and their mother were in the midst of an involved matchmaking plot. Why they felt it necessary to throw her into anyone's company was beyond him. The lady looked quite capable of finding her own willing companions. He numbered himself among the lot and decided that he owed the kids one. "Augustus Octavian Tripopulous."

Nancy, who didn't even have a middle name, much less one that overwhelming, could only stare at him. Slowly her mouth curved upward. "That certainly is a mouthful."

"But he said to call him Guy," Addie injected quickly, eager to eliminate any hurdles for her mother. Maybe Mommy didn't like long names.

"My friends call me Guy," he explained.

And he obviously wanted to be friends, Nancy

thought. Well, her dance card was full. She had all the friends she wanted to have.

"Guy?" she repeated. It didn't seem to follow.

"My sister couldn't say my name when she was little. All she could manage was Guy. It stuck." He was still waiting for her to take his hand.

Nancy's handshake was quick, formal. Perfunctory. "Nice to meet you, Guy."

Mommy didn't mean that, Addie thought, distressed that their plans were falling apart. She knew when Mommy was just being polite.

"She's Nancy," Addie told Guy, when her mother didn't make an attempt to tell him her name.

What was wrong with Mommy? Why wasn't she talking? Guy was so nice, and he had come to her rescue, even if she didn't need to be rescued. That had to mean something to Mommy, didn't it?

"Nancy," Guy repeated slowly. He smiled at her. She looked a little uneasy, and he wondered if he was doing that to her, or if she was just embarrassed about the twins' machinations. "Nice name. And nice kids."

Most people were a little overwhelmed by her twins. She supposed it was a point in his favor that he wasn't.

"I like them," she replied slowly, alluding to the fact that right now, they were not exactly sharing most-favored-child status. "But I am sorry if they inconvenienced you."

Nancy looked around, suddenly realizing that

there was someone missing. Where was Summer, anyway?

"No, actually, they rather brightened what was shaping up to be an otherwise very dull day." Guy looked down at his swimming trunks. "I was just sitting by the pool."

Nancy nodded, unable to resist allowing her gaze to shift over him again. He had to get his uniform tailor-made, she decided. Uniform shirts didn't come tapered, certainly not enough to accommodate his build. "That would explain the tan."

"What?" He'd been indoors and in his car far more than he was happy about of late. But he supposed that to the undiscerning eye he did look as if he had a deep suntan. "Oh, no, that's mostly my complexion. I don't get much of a chance to get down to the beach, or the pool. This is actually my first day off in about a month."

Guilt resurrected itself. "And they interrupted you." She looked reprovingly at her children. They knew how she felt about them bothering people.

He didn't want her blaming Addie and A.J. He'd gotten a kick out of what they were obviously up to. It reminded him of something he and Demi might have tried to pull at the twins' age.

"I like my work," he told her quickly. "And Addie and A.J. actually entertained me by giving me a mystery close to home."

She could be regarded as a mystery, he thought. Because it was certainly a mystery to him why someone who looked like Nancy Douglas was un-attached. If she was attached, the twins wouldn't be looking at him as if he were the last ice-cream cone for two hundred miles.

"Hey, are we having, like, a party here?" Summer, her long blond hair swaying against her shoulders, sauntered into the kitchen.

A distant flushing noise answered Nancy's question about where Summer had been the past few minutes. But not the one about how the twins had managed to leave the apartment without her noticing in the first place.

"No, we are not." Nancy pressed her lips together, trying to remember what it had been like to be Summer's age.

She decided that she had never been Summer's age. The oldest of five, she'd never been allowed to be irresponsible. There had always been something to do, someone to look after. She was going to have to find a new baby-sitter. Summer, it was apparent, was destined to go off in other directions.

"Yes," Addie and A.J. chimed in unison, contradicting her. "We are." They looked at Guy hopefully, then sneaked another look at their mother.

Coming to the rescue was something that was second nature to him. He moved in closer to the twins, laying a hand on each shoulder.

"I tell you what, let's compromise." Eagerness lit up each small face, though they probably didn't know what the word *compromise* meant. He took that as a vote of confidence in him. He raised his eyes to Nancy's to gauge her reaction. So far, he couldn't tell. She'd be a fair hand at poker, if she played, he decided. "Let's celebrate your mother's escape from the kidnappers."

"Kidnappers?" Summer echoed, her eyes as wide as the medallion she wore around her neck. "Hey, cool."

Definitely a new sitter. "No, Summer, not cool," Nancy said wearily. "Not cool at all."

Nancy dug into her purse and took out the last of her spare cash. There was just enough to cover what she owed Summer. More than enough, if she paid the teenager what she was worth. She had to remember to stop at the bank tomorrow and cash her check.

"Here." Nancy pressed the bills into Summer's hand, as she ushered her toward the door. "I won't be needing you anymore."

Summer slid the money into the front pocket of her jeans. How, Nancy had no idea. There didn't seem to be enough room left for a breath, much less money. "You mean today."

"Yes, today." Nancy closed the front door behind Summer. "Or ever," she added, rather audibly, under her breath. Turning, she blew out a breath, her gaze sweeping over her children. Where did she begin? "What were you thinking? You know I don't want you running around outside by yourselves."

To her annoyance, Addie and A.J. seemed to

close ranks around their newfound friend. It was almost as if they were forming an alliance, one that she wasn't very happy about.

The kids were gathering around him, as if he were their protector, Guy thought. That would cast Nancy in the role of the heavy. The image tickled his sense of humor.

"This is a very safe city," Guy told her mildly, "and they were staying close to home. They only went out as far as the pool."

"Yeah!" A.J. cried, relieved to be championed. "The pool. And we had to get Guy."

"Officer Tripopulous." She didn't think it was right for them to be on a first-name basis with an adult. "And you didn't have to get him," Nancy reminded her son. "I wasn't—"

Guy saw distress mirrored on two small faces. It was obvious they didn't want to be embarrassed in front of him. He diverted Nancy's attention.

"They can call me Guy," he assured her. "I don't mind. Now…" Easing away from the twins, he approached her. "If you give me a few minutes to change, we can go out and begin our celebration."

Even if she wanted to go, she couldn't. Nancy shook her head. "I'm sorry, I just gave the last of my money to Summer."

He wasn't about to let her get out of it that easily. Not when so much planning had gone into getting the two of them together. He glanced at the twins. "My treat."

She wasn't in the habit of allowing herself to be picked up by strange men, even if it was in the middle of her own kitchen.

"I don't even know you."

"Yes, you do, Mommy," Addie insisted.

Why was Mommy saying no? She was going to ruin everything, Addie thought. He was being really nice to them, and she liked the way he smelled. Kind of the way Daddy had, she suddenly remembered, as something sad pricked her belly.

Nancy felt as if she were the only salmon trying to swim upstream. She had every right to just politely show the man the door. Still, she raised one brow and looked at him. "I do?"

"Sure, I'm the policeman next door. Your potential rescuer," he added for good measure.

"What he said," A.J. chimed in. Addie wasn't the only one who was on the policeman's side, he thought, taking a step closer to the man. And then he looked up at his mother. "Please, Mommy?"

Addie knew that at bottom, Mommy was a softy. She joined ranks with her brother, pouring it on. "Yes, please, Mommy?"

They were quite a team when they got rolling, Guy thought with admiration. Just like he and Demi had been when they used to join forces against their parents. He knew the look on Nancy's face well. She was going to cave any second. Guy added his two cents.

"You can't say no to such eloquent pleas," he pointed out.

Nancy shot a warning look at her children. They were embarrassing her by putting Guy on the spot. "You really don't have to."

Where had she gotten the idea that going out with a woman who had curves that would bring a weak man to his knees was a hardship? Even if she did come accompanied by two very animated accessories.

"But I'd *like* to." She was going to say no—not to her kids, but to him. Guy quickly continued, "I was raised to always be friendly with my neighbors." Knowing he was playing dirty pool, he turned his argument toward the twins. "And you three are my neighbors, have been for over a month. It's time we got to know each other, right, kids?"

A.J. nodded so hard, he was in danger of having his head fall off. "Right."

Addie merely smiled serenely, assured that she had won. "You bet."

Guy turned to Nancy, a satisfied look in his eyes. "I think you're outvoted."

When had this gone up for a vote? "Whatever gave you the idea that this is a democracy, Officer Tripopulous? I run a dictatorship."

Guy clucked in mild disbelief. A.J. giggled. "Shame on you, Nancy—this is what America is all about. Freedom of choice. Any time you'd like to come over, my grandmother would be more than happy to tell you all about what it means not to have any.''

She couldn't even begin to spell his last name, and he was already bringing her around to meet his grandmother. The man certainly didn't let grass grow under *his* feet. The humorist in her kicked in. Nancy was beginning to see a potential column evolving here. ''She's from the old country?''

''Yes, and from the old man.'' He grinned, then explained, ''My grandfather. A tyrant if ever there was one.''

The affection in his voice told her that if Guy did think of his grandfather as a tyrant, the man was a benevolent one.

Guy was smiling at her again. It was one of those completely disarming smiles that made a woman temporarily abandon common sense. For a second, Nancy forgot to make mental notes for her column.

And then she roused herself. Maybe an outing wasn't such a bad idea after all.

Besides, until she walked through the door, she'd been running on empty as far as an idea for her next column went. Writing humor had become a very serious business since she began to do it for a living. ''My Safe Escape from the Kidnappers.'' That would be her working title, Nancy decided, until a better one hit her.

''All right,'' Nancy agreed, ''I suppose we could celebrate my safe return.'' ''My Safe Return.'' That might be a better title, she thought. ''There's a little soda shop at the outdoor mall a few miles from here.''

They'd be in and out of there in under half an hour. And now that he'd gotten the lady to agree, Guy wanted to go somewhere where they could spend at least an hour in each other's company, if not more.

''Actually,'' he said, hedging, ''I was thinking of something a little more substantial—''

Or ''How I Drowned in the Policeman Next Door's Eyes.'' That would be an even better title. At least it was more accurate than the other two.

Nancy looked away. ''I'd rather not go to a fancy restaurant with them.'' *Or you,* she added silently.

Guy laughed. ''Demi will be very happy to hear it referred to that way.''

She frowned. ''Demi?'' The name meant nothing to her. But then, neither had his ten minutes ago.

He was getting ahead of himself. But there was something about Nancy Douglas that had him running instead of walking.

''My sister. She runs the restaurant now. The family restaurant,'' he clarified. ''My grandparents started it, passed it on to my father, and then he passed it on to us. Except that I didn't see myself behind the counter. Demi was the one in the family who could run a business and didn't mind being in one place for thirty hours a day.''

A.J. tugged on his arm. When Guy looked down,

he saw the uncertainty in the boy's eyes. Eyes like his mother's, Guy thought.

"There's only twenty-four hours in a day," he whispered solemnly.

Guy tried very hard not to smile. "My mistake."

Someone else would have taken offense at being corrected by a child, Nancy thought. Julian had thought children belonged on another planet. It had turned out that Julian was the one who belonged there, at least in her opinion. The sports columnist had offered her a shoulder to cry on when Tom was killed in the line of duty. She'd been so lost, she actually thought that was all the man was offering.

If she hadn't been so off balance, she would have realized that Julian was only trying to move in on her while she was vulnerable. She'd set him straight soon enough. And set herself straight in the bargain.

Tom was gone, and it was up to her to take care of their children. There wasn't any time to indulge in self-pity, and there certainly wasn't any time to allow herself to be vulnerable.

So, from that day forward, she hadn't been. Not being vulnerable meant not being susceptible to a pair of eyes green enough to be mistaken for grass or shoulders wide enough to dive off.

Still, Addie and A.J. were looking at her so hopefully, it was hard to say no. It had been a while since they went anywhere. Work had kept her busier than any of them liked—except, of course, for the bill collector. Looking into those little faces, she couldn't find it in her heart to turn them down.

"All right." Addie and A.J. cheered as she capitulated. "Family restaurant it is."

Guy winked at the twins as he passed them. *I owe you one,* he thought. "I'll be right back," he promised Nancy, leaving.

As soon as the door closed behind Guy, Nancy turned around and faced her two matchmakers. Instead of saying anything, she unfolded the note in her hand, then studied it. She could hear the twins shifting uncomfortably as they waited.

She raised her eyes to her daughter. "Your penmanship could stand improving, Addie."

Addie lowered her head, contrite. She knew Mommy never got mad if she was sorry. "Yes, Mommy."

Nancy's lips twitched. The little actress. She held up the paper. "Whose idea was this, anyway?"

Addie bit her lower lip. "Well..."

"It was mine!" A.J. cried out, before his sister could say anything. He wasn't about to let Addie take the blame. And after all, he *was* the one who had watched the movie and come up with the idea in the first place.

Addie moved closer to A.J., as if to protect him. "But we both agreed on it."

Nancy's heart swelled. How could she be angry with them when they acted like this?

"Well, at least you're both loyal to each other. I

suppose that's something." And then she smiled, and they knew it was going to be all right. "I guess I can't expect those creative little genes of yours to lie around dormant with nothing to do, can I?"

A.J. shook his head in reply, though he wasn't really sure what Mommy was talking about.

Nancy looked at the paper again. "But why kidnapping?"

"He's a policeman," Addie explained. "We knew he would want to help."

Nancy laughed. If there was just a way to tap into this energy, maybe she wouldn't be struggling so hard to write these days. "I guess it could have been worse. You could have said I was murdered."

"Oh, no, Mommy." A.J. laughed. "Then he couldn't date you." As soon as the words were out, A.J. covered his mouth, but it was too late.

Oh, sweetie, I don't need a man in my life. I have you and your sister. Nancy threaded her arms around her son and then Addie.

"And he's not dating me now, A.J. We're just going out to be neighborly, nothing else. Got it?" She looked at him to make sure he understood.

He nodded his head, albeit reluctantly. "Got it."

She looked at Addie. The deal wasn't sealed unless her little ringleader went along with it. "You?"

Addie nodded her head, echoing her brother. "Got it, Mommy."

"Good." If she was going out, she had better

freshen up. No sense in looking like something the cat dragged in, just because this wasn't a date.

As soon as Nancy walked away, Addie poked A.J. in the ribs. Hard.

Doubling over, he clutched his side. "What was that for?" he hissed.

"For telling." She had to watch him every minute, or he'd spoil everything. She supposed it was all up to her now. Boys were so hopelessly babyish.

"I'm sorry," he said. "But she is going out with him."

Addie smiled. The thought made her feel happy all over. "Yeah, she is."

"Addie? How long do you think it'll be before they get married?"

"A long time. At least two weeks," she replied solemnly.

A.J. sighed. Two weeks was a long time to wait for a daddy.

3

---➤◀---

Relief washed over Demi.

It always did whenever she saw her older brother walk through the doors of the Parthenon restaurant. Not that she would tell him, of course, but she worried about him. A great deal.

She supposed it was in the genes, a holdover from when they'd been very young and she'd thought him a complete idiot, challenged by the task of putting his shoes on the right feet. That had been because Mom and Grandma tended to baby Guy, making him, in her opinion, good for absolutely nothing and capable of accomplishing nothing. It had been her sworn duty to show him that he wasn't a miniature god, but a pain-in-the-butt brother.

In her opinion, she'd done a pretty good job.

But things had grown a great deal more complicated since they were seven and nine. Now she actually had a reason to worry about him. Guy was a policeman, and although the city they lived in ranked as one of safest cities in the country for its size, she couldn't help feeling anxious about his safety. It took only one crazy gunman firing one well-aimed shot to bring someone's life to an end. And blue made such an easy target.

Exchanging final pleasantries with the people she had just shown to their table, Demi excused herself and worked her way back to the hostess's desk.

So who was this? she wondered. The woman he had in tow did not look like Guy's usual choice for a dining companion. The trim blonde was definitely not of the lightweight, blow-away-in-the-wind-intelligence variety Demi was accustomed to seeing with Guy.

Well, well, well, looks like Mom's lectures are finally taking hold, she thought, pleased. She was tired of waiting to become an aunt.

Demi's smile faded when she saw two children in the woman's wake. Disappointment nudged its way to the surface. The woman wasn't a date. Obviously, this was just someone he was helping out. Guy was like that, always bringing home strays.

As he grew up, he'd graduated from stray dogs and cats to stray people. This one was rather nicely dressed for a stray. But strays came from all walks of life. Demi wondered what the woman's problem was, and if she needed a job, like the last person Guy had brought to her. That had been Brady, and he'd had amnesia at the time. Against all odds, that scenario had turned out rather well for everyone concerned.

With luck, Demi thought, so would this, although

right now she really wasn't in a position to offer anyone a job at the restaurant. There wasn't enough work at times to keep even her occupied.

Guy saw Demi approaching and inclined his head toward the twins. "See the woman making a beeline for us?" He nodded in her direction. "That's my sister. Don't get scared, kids," he said as Demi joined them. "She always looks like that."

Demi stuck her tongue out at Guy and then smiled serenely at his companions. Her face did a complete transformation from that of a mischievous, amusing green-eyed woman to that of the sophisticated owner of a three-generations-old restaurant.

She hardly looked like the same woman. Nancy was impressed, her brain racing off in two directions as she made mental notes. So far, this was great fodder for her column.

And to think, she'd been worried about finding something to write about.

Demi looked at her brother's newest conquests. The kids looked like their mom, she decided. "Welcome to the Parthenon. What can I get for you?"

Moving past his sister, Guy began to lead the way into the main room. There were murals on two sides of the walls, depicting the Olympic Games. He noted that the twins were staring at them, awestruck.

"A table, for starters," he said to Demi as he shook his head. "Didn't they teach you anything in that fancy restaurant school besides how to order expensive wine?"

In an attempt to upgrade the restaurant, Demi had wanted to expand their wine cellar and ordered bottles of outrageously expensive wine that no one bought. It had been her first and only mistake when she took over the helm of the restaurant. Demi figured Guy would remind her of it until the day one of them died.

"Yes," she answered crisply, "they taught me how to get rid of deadbeats."

Getting the jump on his sister, A.J. asked, "What's a deadbeat?" throwing the question open to any of the three adults around him.

Demi was quicker than Guy. She always had been. "Someone who thinks he can eat for free." She stopped at a booth, her brother's favorite. During the busy times, it was always the last she filled, in case he dropped by. Of late, keeping it empty hadn't been a problem. "Out to impress someone with your largess?" she asked Guy sweetly.

"Not by bringing them to you."

Guy shepherded the two children in front of him as if he were an old hand at this, Demi thought. Maybe this *was* someone who counted. Demi stole a glance at the woman's left hand, and was disappointed again. There was a plain gold band on it.

She looked down at the small boy about to snake his way into the booth. "I'm Demi. What's your name?"

Proud to be asked ahead of his sister, he lifted his chin. "A.J."

Addie pushed her brother into the booth and slid in next. She looked directly into Demi's eyes. "Addie."

Demi recognized a kindred spirit and smiled broadly. She shook each of their hands solemnly.

"Please to meet you, A.J. and Addie. You've come at a good time." She gestured toward the booth. "Our finest booth just happens to be free."

Guy looked around. The room had a capacity of three hundred. Less than twenty occupied the tables and booths. "Looks like most of your booths are free. Bad day?"

She knew it was stupid to be defensive, especially with Guy, but she was very possessive when it came to the restaurant. Any shortcomings reflected directly on her.

"No, just a lull. Don't worry about it." She handed each child a menu, then slipped one to Nancy. "Guy has obviously forgotten his manners. How do you do? I'm Demi Tripopulous, Guy's sister."

Nancy looked at the snapping green eyes, the torrent of black hair and the easy, winning smile. The resemblance was impossible to miss. And, she had to admit, hard to resist. "Hi, I'm Nancy Douglas, Guy's neighbor."

Demi stole a look at her brother. "Oh."

It was a very pregnant "Oh," and Nancy felt as if she had just had First Prize stamped on her forehead by some large, invisible machine. She stopped doing a rough draft in her head and began paying closer attention to what was actually happening here.

It didn't take five years on the force and a carefully honed ability for creating psychological profiles for Guy to see what was going on. Much as the lady interested him, he wasn't going to get anywhere if Demi scared her off.

"Antennae down, Demi, we're here celebrating Nancy's safe return from the kidnappers. Right, kids?" He slid into the booth beside Nancy.

"Right!" the twins echoed.

Demi's brows drew together as she looked at Nancy. "Oh?"

Nancy sighed. "It's a long story."

Demi folded her arms before her. "I like long stories. I grew up with a Greek grandfather." She leaned over toward Nancy. "You'll have to tell it to me sometime."

Guy tugged playfully on the edge of Demi's short lacy apron. She looked at him impatiently.

"Don't you have inventory to take or something?" he asked.

Demi looked at Addie and rolled her eyes. "Brothers."

"Yeah, brothers," Addie repeated, mimicking Demi's tone to a T. She was pleased to have found an adult who actually shared her feelings on the subject.

"You and I are going to have to stick together," Guy said to A.J.

A.J. nodded, eager to bond with Guy, then stopped as he looked at his mother with true concern. "Who'll stick with Mommy?"

Nancy had an uneasy feeling she knew who would volunteer for that duty, and she wanted to set things straight before any misunderstandings evolved.

"Mommy is doing just fine on her own, A.J.," she said pointedly. "Don't worry about me."

Demi looked at Guy, raising her brow in a silent question. Guy gave no indication that he had even heard Nancy's comment.

But he had. Loud and clear. Well, that certainly put him in his place, Guy thought. Still, he'd always enjoyed a challenge. The greater the challenge, the sweeter the prize.

But there'd be no prize if they all starved to death. He looked at his sister. "Hey, don't I get a menu?"

She patted his shoulder. Guy had worked here all through high school. Very little had changed after she felt her way around that first year she took over.

"This is Tuesday, Guy. No surprises." She turned toward her brother's guests. "Take your time, and I'll be by to take your order in a few minutes." Smiling, she retreated.

Addie looked after Demi, still feeling special for having been singled out. "She's nice."

Yes, Demi had her moments, he thought. "She bakes a mean pastry," Guy told the little girl.

Guy made it sound as if it were a good thing. A.J.

was confused. "Why do you want a paste that's mean?"

Nancy struggled not to laugh. A.J. tended to be very literal. "It's an expression, honey," she explained. "Guy means that it's very good."

"Paste?" A.J. was still mystified.

"No, pastry," Guy corrected. "It's cake."

A.J.'s eyes lit up. Cake was something he understood. "Oh, boy."

A.J.'s enthusiasm was always infectious. Nancy grinned. "Yeah—oh, boy." She set down her menu. "Everything looks so good," she told Guy. "Any suggestions?"

Several came to mind. But they didn't have anything to do with what the kitchen was serving up. He smiled into her eyes.

"A few."

Something warm shimmied through her. No, absolutely no warm shimmying, she told herself sternly. "On the menu," she said, prompting him.

"Oh, that, too." A smile was in his eyes, Nancy realized a moment before he slid closer to her. "You mind sharing your menu for a second?" He reached for it. "Demi has an annoying gift called total recall and just assumes everyone else does, too." Guy scanned the menu, then smiled. "Why not try the shepherd's pie?" Demi's chef followed their grandmother's recipe. His grandfather was fond of saying strong men wept for a taste.

"Is it good?" A.J. asked eagerly.

"Melts in your mouth," Guy assured him, slipping the menu back to Nancy.

"Lots of things melt in A.J.'s mouth," Addie said disdainfully. "He eats sloppy."

"Do not," A.J. piped up. He looked miserable enough to die.

Yup, just like Demi and him, Guy thought fondly, commiserating with his counterpart.

"Addie," Nancy said sharply. She didn't like Addie humiliating her brother at home, and she particularly frowned on it when they were out in public. "Remember where we are."

"Sorry, Mommy." Addie looked properly chastised—for an entire minute and a half, by Guy's watch.

He had to hand it to Nancy. "My mother could have stood to take lessons from you. Demi and I were always at it."

She thought of the exchange she'd just witnessed between Guy and his sister. "Doesn't seem to have changed much."

He dismissed what she'd seen with a wave of his hand. "That was nothing—she could have phoned that in." Memory had a habit of taking past events and painting them in progressively softer colors as time elapsed. He could smile about it now. It hadn't been that easy then. "Demi was a holy terror. It's not something that's easily overcome."

"And you're crazy about her." That much was

obvious to Nancy. Maybe there was hope for Addie and A.J. after all.

He leaned in toward her. "Lower your voice. She's not supposed to know that." Nancy laughed, and Guy leaned back in his seat, studying her. "That's nice."

Something skittered through her on tiny, nervous feet. "What is?"

"Your laugh." It was deep and throaty and sexy as all hell.

"I can laugh like a donkey. Wanna hear me?" A.J. asked, then winced as he felt a sharp rap on his shin. "Ow." Rubbing his leg, A.J. looked accusingly at his sister who gave him a hard, silencing look. She mouthed the word *Mommy*. It took him a minute before he understood.

When he did, he retreated, falling into silence. A.J. had gotten carried away with Guy's company and forgotten that they had to get Mommy to really like the policeman first. This was a date. Addie had explained it all to him when they began to cast around for a plan earlier this week. And on a date, he wasn't supposed to talk too much, but it was hard, because he liked Guy a lot.

"Go ahead," Guy said encouragingly.

"Um, I forgot how." Two hands wrapped around his water glass, A.J. brought the rim close to his mouth and took a long sip.

A.J. looked uncomfortable, Guy thought. Maybe

he should have taken them to the soda shop. "How about a cola with a cherry in it?"

"Yeah!" Addie forgot to remain demure, and echoed A.J.'s cry of enthusiasm.

Guy looked around for Demi, but she was busy at another table. He slid out of the booth.

"Wait right here. Two colas coming up," he said. Nancy could stand to be put at ease a little herself, he judged. "Can I get you anything?"

She was busy mentally drafting her column, and it took her a minute to actually hear the question. "Oh, a cola would be nice," she murmured absently.

"Three," he amended, leaving.

As soon as he walked away, the twins moved closer to their mother. She had the distinct impression that she was being laid siege to.

"Isn't he nice, Mommy?" A.J. asked.

God, they were so transparent, Nancy thought. But then, at eight, maybe she had been, too. And they had been through so much. It wasn't easy growing up without a father, even in the nineties.

"Yes," she allowed. "He's very nice."

Addie sighed dramatically. "You know, when I grow up, I hope I find someone as nice as Guy."

Nancy raised an amused eyebrow. Talk about laying it on thick. "Play your cards right, and Guy might still be available."

A.J. was confused. "You gotta play cards?"

Nancy laughed. She could have hugged him, but

at eight, he was trying to carve out a scrap of independence for himself, at least out in public, where some of his friends might see him. That meant no hugging once they were outside the apartment.

"Sometimes." She looked at her little matchmakers. They really could do a job on her heartstrings. "Kids, don't get any ideas. We're just here because he's our neighbor and I feel guilty after what you did to him."

Addie was quick to wiggle out of any blame. "We didn't do anything to him."

Nancy pinned her daughter with a long look. "You lied to him."

A.J. hung his head for his part in the plot. "It was a little lie. And he said it gave him a misty—"

"Mystery," Addie corrected crisply, sparing him an exasperated look.

How had Addie managed to get so old so fast? Nancy wondered. She saw a great deal of herself in her daughter. Still, she had never tried to spin devious plots around her mother.

She hadn't had to, Nancy reminded herself. Her father had still been alive. Addie and A.J.'s wasn't.

Nancy placed a hand over each of theirs on the table. "I know it's hard on you sometimes, kids, not having a father. It's hard on me, too—"

Addie saw her opportunity and jumped right in. "That's why Guy is so great. He likes us. And I can see he really likes you, Mommy—"

She could feel the butter being slathered on her

with a shovel. Nancy had trouble maintaining a straight face. "Oh, you do, do you?"

"Yeah," A.J. concurred. "His eyes get all shiny when he looks at you. Just like when that man saw the lady on the airplane—"

Nancy held up a hand. "Hold it. What man? What airplane?"

It took A.J. a minute to get his bearings. He'd been going full steam ahead. "On TV."

Nancy rolled her eyes. TV again. "We have *got* to get you away from the television set, A.J. My fault." She took full responsibility for this. Reap what ye sow, she thought. "I've let the TV be your baby-sitter far too long."

There was no denying that it made her feel safe, while she was at the computer, searching for a column to rise up out of the keyboard, to hear the sound of the television set in the background and know that her kids were sitting there watching, safe and out of harm's way. She supposed that had its roots in Tom's being killed, but it was still a difficult thing to shake. And, obviously, it came with a price.

A.J. pouted. "TV's better than having ol' Summer around."

"No argument there," she heartily agreed. Then she smiled, running a hand over his hair. "We'll talk about it, okay?"

"'Kay," A.J. agreed.

* * *

Demi walked into the kitchen, looking for Guy. She'd seen him enter a minute ago. He was at the soda dispenser.

"What are you doing back here?" she wanted to know.

In the background, the afternoon chef raised and lowered his shoulders in an exaggerated shrug, indicating that he had no clue why her brother was helping himself to three glasses and a tray and playing waiter.

"What does it look like I'm doing?" Filling it, Guy placed the last glass on the tray and looked around for the jar of cherries. "I'm helping myself." The jar was in the center of the toppings tray. Guy distributed two cherries in each glass of cola. "Service is terrible. I'm thinking of complaining to the manager."

He knew she didn't like him getting underfoot. They had an agreement. She didn't come down to the precinct and riffle through his reports, he didn't roam around her kitchen. Usually.

"You are complaining to the manager, and the manager doesn't like customers helping themselves."

Guy picked up the tray. "Improve your service, and I won't have to."

Her edgy temper was getting the best of her again, she thought ruefully. It wasn't Guy's fault that business had fallen off. Demi took three straws and placed them on the tray. She didn't want to argue with Guy.

"She looks nice."

He grinned, pleased by the comment. "She is nice. Got great kids, too." He laughed, and she looked at him, waiting. Resting an edge of the tray against the table, he let her in on the joke. "They came up with a plot about their mother being kidnapped just to get me to come over."

Suspicion reared its head. Guy didn't have a clue how devious women could be. "Sure that she wasn't in on it?"

He knew how Demi's mind worked. "If she was, she's one hell of an actress." To satisfy Demi, he thought about it for a minute and came to the same conclusion. "No, Nancy was too surprised, and then too annoyed with them to have been in on it. They're a crack-up." Amusement curved his mouth. "Remind you of anyone?"

She shrugged. "You, maybe. I was a saint."

Not by any stretch of the imagination. "When did you start losing your memory?"

"Same time you did," she countered dryly. Demi put her hand out, palm up, as if expecting to have something placed in it. "When are you going to pay up? You haven't made a contribution in almost a year. This isn't your private club, you know. We have to turn a profit. I've got parents and grandparents to think of, remember?"

It was a running joke. She liked putting the screws to him. He liked teasing her about her love life. They got along just fine. "I'm family, remember?"

Parting just outside the swinging door, she winced as if in physical pain. "I try to forget that whenever possible."

"Hey, Demi." The serious note in his voice had her turning around again. "Things bad?"

Yeah, they were. Temporarily. But it wasn't anything she couldn't handle.

"Couldn't be better," she replied cheerfully, shooing him off. "Go, bring the sodas out to your fans before they come to their senses and run off. I'll be at the table in a couple of minutes." She held up her hand in response to the skeptical look on his face. "Scout's honor."

He hooted. "You were never a Girl Scout."

She gave him a droll look. "Didn't say I was. They've still got honor, right?"

He merely shook his head and walked toward his booth. There was no such thing as getting in the last word with Demi.

He set the tray on the table, distributing the sodas. "Here we go, three colas, six cherries." He placed the empty tray on a nearby table.

Nancy stripped off the paper around her straw. "I get cherries, too?"

"You look like the cherry type."

Addie's eyes widened. "He guessed, Mommy!" she cried. It was a sign. It had to be. "She likes to sit and eat a whole jar of them when she watches TV," Addie confided eagerly to Guy.

Nancy didn't like being discussed when she was

sitting right here. "Less fattening than potato chips," she explained flippantly. Actually, what drew her to them was a sweet tooth for candied cherries, but she didn't feel like admitting to a weakness right now.

He slid into the booth beside her again. "I'll have to pass that on to Demi when I get a chance. She likes to eat like a horse."

A.J. frowned, trying to remember. "She doesn't look like a horse."

Having referred to her as a pain in the butt didn't mean he wasn't willing to give Demi her due. "That's because she works like one, too. Demi took over when my father got sick," he told Nancy. "Had a real flair for it. So much so that she finished college at night and used her business degree to help get us back on our feet again." While there was always enough to eat, they'd almost gone bankrupt when his father ran the restaurant. Demi had proved to be a lot tougher businesswoman than their father was, for all his bluster. "My father had a habit of carrying a lot of people. He'd charge them whatever they could pay, or just wrote it off." Everyone who was down on his luck always knew there was a warm meal waiting at the Parthenon. Guy had taken pride in that.

Nancy smiled. Guy came from good people. "Sounds like a nice man."

"And nice men have nice children," Addie

he'd do all right. The boy seemed rather sensitive to him, and sensitive people were at risk of being run right over, unless they stood up for themselves. He'd had his grandfather to help him, Guy remembered. Maybe it was time to pass on the favor.

Straining against the seat belt that cut into her waist, Addie wrapped her hands around the back of her mother's seat. "Can I have the key, Mommy?"

"Key?" This was a first. Addie had never asked for the key to the apartment before.

Addie nodded importantly. She knew Guy was never going to kiss Mommy if she and A.J. were around. It was time to disappear.

"I'm a big girl now, Mommy." Her excitement and the pitch of her voice escalated as Guy pulled into his designated parking stall. "I can unlock the door. And I can take care of A.J., too."

Her search for keys on hold, Nancy raised her eyes from her purse. Addie wasn't satisfied inventing kidnappers? Now she was plotting something else? Nancy was almost afraid to ask what.

"I can take care of myself," A.J. protested, a little uneasy about what Addie might have in mind.

He wouldn't have told anyone, but Addie was stronger than he was. He and Addie each had their reasons for wanting a daddy. His was that he needed a daddy to show him how to get stronger than his sister. Guy looked pretty strong. Guy would know what he had to do, A.J. thought hopefully.

Besides, he liked the way Guy looked at Mommy.

Just like Jimmy's daddy looked at his mommy, and they held hands and went to the park every Sunday. A.J. really wanted to go to the park with his very own daddy.

Amused and more than a little curious, Nancy held her keys aloft. Addie snatched them into her hand. But Nancy held on to the ring, her eyes on her daughter's. "Why would you need to take care of A.J.?"

Freed of the seat belt, Addie was already opening the rear door on her side. She gave her mother an impatient look. Was she going to have to help Mommy with everything?

"So you can stay outside and talk to Guy." She saw the look her mother gave her, and quickly tried to correct herself. But "Guy" was a lot easier for her to manage than his last name. It had at least a million letters in it. That it might be her last name if her plan worked hadn't really occurred to Addie yet. "I mean, um, Officer Tripi—Tri…um…" Not to be defeated by a simple stumbling block, she went around it. "So you can talk together."

Key in hand, Addie dragged A.J. in her wake as she snaked out of the car. A.J. tried to move fast, but it wasn't fast enough for Addie. She pulled harder on his arm.

"Ow!" The cry of protest and pain was out before he could think to stop it. He knew big boys didn't whine, and he wanted Guy to think he was a big boy.

"Baby," Addie muttered under her breath, still smiling brightly at her mother and Guy. As soon as his feet hit the ground, Addie grabbed A.J.'s hand and began pulling him toward their apartment. "Take your time," she sang out over her shoulder.

Guy was at her car door, opening it for her, before Nancy could reach for it. Addie's behavior had thrown her off. Nancy flushed as she got out. She and Addie were going to have to have a long talk. A very long talk.

"Not very obvious, are they?"

Guy raised his eyebrows innocently as he locked his doors. "Were they obvious?"

She liked his smile. On a scale of one to ten, it was an easy ten, maybe even higher. And there was no rating his eyes. They were beautiful, and went right off the number chart.

But she wasn't in the market for a smile that created minor ripples in her stomach or eyes that a woman could roam around in for hours. Been there, done that, she insisted silently.

At the very most, she was in the market for a good neighbor. Someone who could look in on her kids if there was an emergency. Anything else was simply out of the question.

She had no idea what had gotten into Addie. A.J., Nancy assumed, had just gotten caught in the undertow. He usually did.

Feeling fidgety, Nancy wrapped her hands around

her purse and held it to her as if it were a security blanket. "Thank you for tolerating them."

He didn't feel like ending this just yet, and everything about her body language told him that she wasn't about to invite him in.

Guy decided to take his cue from Addie, bless her.

Very lightly, he touched his hand to Nancy's elbow and directed her steps toward the small manmade stream that ran through the complex. There was a little wooden footbridge spanning it, not too far from where they were. A gazebo just large enough for two had recently been added. He had an urge to see her sitting in it.

"Hey, I meant what I said. They're very entertaining." He grinned. "They bring back a lot of memories, although Addie is almost laid-back compared to what Demi was like."

Nancy laughed. "I can't imagine anyone making Addie look laid-back."

"Trust me, Demi could have. I barely got out of my early years alive."

He stopped by the gazebo, allowing Nancy to walk in first. The smell of freshly varnished wood mixed with the scent of wildflowers and the light perfume she was wearing. He found the combination arousing.

Nancy sat down, but he remained standing. He had the vague impression that he might scare her off if he sat down beside her. "They're great kids."

He meant that, she thought, and she liked him for it. "Thanks."

He decided to press the temporary grace he'd bought himself. "Been raising them alone long?"

The wary look that entered her eyes came immediately. So, he thought, not only was Mommy embarrassed by her kids' plotting, she really didn't want it yielding any fruit.

Guy leaned back against the railing. "I know I'm prying, but as a cop, I've developed this insatiable curiosity about everything. Or maybe," he added when she didn't answer, "I became a cop to give me an excuse for my insatiable curiosity."

The brook was babbling thanks to a man-made apparatus. Man-made or not, it was a soothing sound. Nancy let it wash over her. Maybe saying the words wouldn't hurt this time.

She shrugged. "Too long."

"You're still wearing your wedding ring. Yes, I noticed," he added, answering the unspoken question in her eyes. "Those keen cop instincts again," he added. "Widow?" he guessed.

Widow. Such an ugly word. It didn't begin to explain the feelings that the state evoked. The emptiness that came with it.

Nancy nodded.

Rising to her feet, she joined him at the railing, looking down into the brook. You could see the bottom, she thought absently. You could see the bottom of a lot of things.

Then, just as the silence was beginning to run a tad too long to be considered comfortable any longer, she added, "He was a policeman, like you." Nancy looked at him. "Tom Douglas."

He would have liked to tell her that he had known her husband, or that he had at least heard of him. People usually found things like that comforting. But the name meant nothing to him. There had been no Tom Douglas on the Bedford force, as far as he knew.

"What precinct did he work out of?"

"Not here." If he'd been here, Tom would still be alive. "He was on the force in East L.A."

Her mouth twitched in a sad smile that hardly managed to curve her lips. Guy had the urge to put his arm around her in mute sympathy, but refrained. She might not have interpreted it correctly. And with reason. Because it wasn't purely altruistic feelings motivating him. There was something else, something small and nameless, beginning to develop.

"Said he wanted to be where he could do the most good." She wished she would have been more vocal back then. Maybe she could have talked Tom out of it. Other places needed policemen. He didn't have to go into the roughest neighborhoods to make a difference.

Spoken like someone who had a true calling, Guy thought.

"Very noble of him," he murmured. He didn't

expect to see the angry light in her eyes when she looked at him.

"No, very selfish of him." It had been a waste, a terrible waste of a good man, who should have lived a long life and then died in bed. Hadn't he owed her that much when he took his vows to be there in sickness and in health? "He should have done the most good for his family, not strangers. He couldn't save the whole world, wouldn't have meant very much to the whole world, but he would have to us. To Addie and A.J. To me." Her quiet tone did little to mask the fierceness of the sentiment she voiced.

Suddenly aware of what she'd said, and to whom, Nancy covered her mouth. "I'm sorry, that just slipped out." She was tired, but that was no excuse. "I don't know what came over me."

He didn't want her apology. He wanted her to feel that she could open up to him. "Sometimes it's good to talk."

Nancy shook her head. "Not when it can't help anything."

He'd been raised not to internalize. His house had been filled with shouting, and with fierce love.

"Oh, I don't know," he said mildly. "They say that confession is good for the soul."

Bemused, she looked at him, and forgot to be embarrassed. "Confession?"

"Confession." Whether she knew it or not, she'd just confessed some of the rage she was trying to deny. "Some schools of thought maintain that anger isn't a good thing to keep locked up inside." He looked at her pointedly.

"I'm not angry," she retorted. "I'm—" Nancy stopped abruptly. What was the use of denying it? He obviously saw through her. Maybe, in a way, she even wanted him to. "Angry," she admitted. "You're right. I'm angry. Angry that he left two children hardly more than babies, angry that he left me."

Guy's eyes touched her face, coaxing the words from her. "What happened?"

She recited the details from the much-folded article she had read and reread over the years. The whole thing had made page 26. Hardly worth the effort for the copy editor.

"A liquor store robbery. Tom was off duty." Her eyes shifted to Guy, irony in her gaze. "Except that a policeman is never off duty, is he? So Tom ran in to save the store owner and his wife. He managed to save them, all right, but he took a bullet for his trouble. Right to the head." She bit her lower lip to keep it from trembling. "Paramedics said he died instantly," she whispered. "At least he didn't feel any pain."

"But you do."

She raised her eyes to his face. She saw nothing but sympathy there. Not pity, but sympathy. He was a cop. He understood.

"Every day of my life, whenever I see our kids.

Whenever I think of what we might have had—''
Color suddenly rose up to her cheeks, halting her
words and adding a blush that was almost irresist-
ible. ''God, you are easy to talk to.''

She wasn't usually vocal about this. About other
things, yes. Talking on paper was her stock-in-trade.
But this belonged to the private Nancy, the one the
world never got to see.

His smile evaporated some of her embarrassment.
''Comes from listening to endless stories as a kid.
My grandfather liked to reminisce, I liked to learn.''

She'd never listened to her grandparents when
they got started talking. She regretted that now, she
thought. ''That's rare in a child.''

Maybe, but for him it had been second nature.
''Fortunately, it worked out.'' He grinned. ''Demi
liked to do a lot of talking, too, in case you hadn't
noticed.''

The mention of his sister brought lunch to mind.
''I wish you'd let me pay for something.'' Except
that her wallet was empty, she remembered. ''I
could write you a check. They ate so much—'' Addie and A.J. both had healthy appetites, but this had
gone beyond anything she was accustomed to. They
had truly pigged out.

She was changing the subject, Guy thought. He
let her. ''Demi was the one who insisted on bringing
out the dessert cart.''

That didn't change anything. ''Yes, but she was

just giving them a choice. They didn't have to eat three desserts apiece.''

Delighted with them, Demi had almost forced the contents of the cart on the duo.

"You're only young once. And at eight, you don't think about calories or getting sick. Let them enjoy it. I know Demi did." This time he did move closer to her. "And so did I."

Too close. Warning flares went up, and she was quick to heed them. "Um, Officer Tripopulous—"

He didn't like the sound of that. "We'll get along a lot better if you start calling me Guy. Granted, it's not the greatest name in the whole world, but it's a lot easier to manage than Tripopulous. And it's a lot better than the other nickname Demi gave me," he added before she could say anything, hoping he had learned enough about double-talk from Demi to keep Nancy from saying something one of them was going to regret.

He'd stopped her cold, arousing her curiosity again. He was good, she thought. Definitely worthy of a column or two, once she got her head together.

"Which is?"

"You realize, of course, that I'm volunteering information that would've had to be gotten out of me only after severe torture when I was younger." He grinned. "When she was angry, Demi took to calling me Octopus—her version of Octavian."

Yes, she could definitely see the dark-haired woman tormenting Guy with that. "I see your point.

All right—Guy," she conceded. "I appreciate your patience with Addie and A.J.—"

Here it comes, he thought, the lady was getting her broom out, ready to give him the brush-off. "I already told you—"

She held up her hand. Demi and Addie, it seemed, weren't the only ones who were versed in fast talk. "There's more."

The sigh was exaggerated. Then he nodded. "I had a feeling."

She really did like him, she thought. But not in any way that could be serious. She refused to ever feel that way about anyone else again. The price was too high. "I'm really not looking to become involved."

Something in her eyes contradicted her words, but he let it go for now. There was no hurry.

"Fair enough." His eyes held hers. "What are you looking for?"

She shrugged, looking away. Before her, the rest of the complex, designed to be pleasing to the eye, spread out in two directions. She watched a toddler pedaling like mad on a chunky yellow-and-blue three-wheeler that hugged the ground. Behind him, his parents followed, arm in arm.

That. I want that.

"That" wasn't an option for her anymore.

"A little peace and quiet once in a while," she answered, studying the tips of her folded fingers. "A steady paycheck that'll help me take care of my kids.'' And then, because she hated being serious for too long, she flashed a grin. ''And once in a while, a good movie on a Saturday night.''

He'd never been slow on the uptake. ''Sounds good to me. I'm free on Saturday night.''

She hadn't been hinting, and quickly regrouped. ''I meant at home, curled up with a tub of microwave popcorn and no shoes.''

It wasn't going to be that easy to get rid of him. ''Even better.''

Tenacious, like a bulldog. She laughed and shook her head. ''You're not going to take no for an answer, are you?''

He believed a relationship had to be built on honesty or it had nowhere to go. ''Not entirely. You do have room for friends in this world of yours that you've fashioned, don't you?''

Friends was a very nice, safe word. Still, she felt herself on shaky ground. ''Well, yes.'' The reply was cautiously given.

''Good.'' Guy nodded. ''It's a start. I like having friends.''

There was something about his manner that made it easy for her to lower her guard. Or maybe, just maybe, she was tired from holding it up for so long. Holding it up against the world. Against everything that might hurt.

Humor did that for her. It kept people at bay and insulated her. As long as she had humor as her weapon, it would be all right.

"So do I."

"All right, then it's agreed. Friends." He put out his hand and waited for her to respond. When she did, he wrapped his fingers around hers, sealing the bargain. They were friends. Step one. Whether step two followed remained to be seen.

Dropping his hand again, Guy nodded in the direction of their apartments. "Maybe we'd better be getting back before Addie has A.J. cleaning up her room."

The comment showed insight. "You *have* been in this situation before."

He waited for her to leave the gazebo first, then followed. The lady, he decided, looked just as good going as she did coming. "I told you, Demi rode roughshod over me for more years than I care to remember."

She couldn't envision anyone ordering him around unless he let them. "I thought you mentioned that she was younger."

"She is." He slipped his hand into hers, taking it as if they'd been walking hand in hand forever. When she didn't try to pull it away, he chalked it up as a point in his favor. "It never stopped her." Debating for a moment, he steered the conversation closer to home. "You got awfully quiet there toward the end of lunch," he noted.

There was something comforting about having him hold her hand this way. Comforting and familiar. Because she suddenly needed that familiarity, however briefly, she let her hand remain where it was.

"I was just remembering," Nancy explained. Her expression softened as she spoke. "It reminded me a great deal of when Tom and I would go out with the kids."

At her door, she turned around to face him. He saw the twinge of hurt in her eyes, even though she tried to hide it. For the first time, he realized how truly vulnerable she was.

"I'm sorry if I brought up any painful memories."

He sounded as if he meant it, and it touched her. It hadn't been her intention to make him feel guilty.

"Don't be. The memories were all very sweet. That period was the very best time in my life."

Guy looked down into her face. God, but she looked sweet. Sweet and sensual at the same time. It was a deadly combination.

He found himself losing ground. "Your life is hardly over, Nancy."

Something caught in her throat and stayed there, stopping her breath as she looked into his eyes. "Sometimes I feel that way." It wasn't just Tom's life that had been cut short by the gunman's bullet. Part of her had died that night, in that run-down liquor store.

Guy had no choice, really. Not when he thought about it.

Except he didn't think. Didn't try to step away.

It wouldn't have helped if he had. It was as if the part of him that controlled his legs were frozen. Instead, he leaned over and did what came as naturally to him as breathing.

The tips of his fingers just barely gliding along her cheek, Guy brushed his lips over hers. An incredibly sweet ache overtook him the moment he did, urging him on, just the slightest bit farther.

Cupping her cheek, touching nothing more than his lips to hers, Guy deepened the kiss a little more. And then still more, until the kindling caught and the fire took on a life of its own.

Enough.

The command almost roared through his brain, ordering him to break away. He'd just finished telling her they were friends. He didn't want Nancy to think that it was a line. And friends didn't force friends to do anything against their will.

Except, he knew in his heart, he hadn't forced this. Hadn't overridden anything but words. Because the woman he was kissing was kissing back. And unless he had suddenly become a very poor judge of character, she wanted this as much as he did.

Something within him sang as he took her into his arms and drew her slowly to him.

Like honey, golden honey, the sensation poured through her, coloring everything it touched. For a moment, she couldn't think, didn't want to. All she wanted to do, for the briefest moment in time, was to feel this, enjoy this, and then she would stop. Stop quickly, before it had any consequences. Before there were any misunderstandings. But until her moment was up, oh, God, until her moment was up, she was going to get lost in this.

Somewhere in the distance, they heard a muffled cheer. It was immediately followed by what sounded like a thud and then a cry of protest.

A.J.'s.

The smile that bloomed simultaneously on both their lips was instrumental in separating them. Turning toward the apartment in unison, they saw the sway of the kitchen curtain as it fell back into place.

Guy laughed, reluctantly releasing her. "I think we had an audience."

There was no question in Nancy's mind. She took a step away from him. "I'd better go and explain to them that this didn't mean anything."

And while I'm at it, I'd better explain that to myself, too.

He lightly placed his hand on her arm. "So, *friend,* Saturday night still open?"

Not a good idea. Not until she had a chance to sort a few things out. "I, um—"

He wasn't going to give her a chance to say no. Guy deliberately kept his tone light. "I'll rent the video, you bring the popcorn."

It did sound like fun. And it would give her a chance to make him realize that there was nothing between them but friendship. "As long as we don't give them the wrong idea."

He looked at her, and she couldn't really read his expression. "We won't."

Something fluttered within her. That was just what she was afraid of. She backed off.

"I'll let you know," Nancy muttered.

Letting herself into her apartment, she held on to the doorknob a little longer than was necessary, testing the integrity of her knees.

They weren't very strong.

Wasn't this supposed to be like riding a bicycle? It had been four years since she was kissed by a man. Since she let a man kiss her.

But the kiss hadn't made her feel like a woman. It had sent her hurtling through time and space, making her feel like a teenager. A teenager being kissed for the very first time. Back to square one.

You would have thought, after putting in her dues, that the experiences she'd garnered along the way would be cumulative.

Well, they weren't.

5

Two seconds after she entered the apartment, Nancy found herself surrounded and outnumbered.

A.J. tugged on her arm, vying for attention first. "So when are we getting married?" Eagerness burst out of every syllable.

"*We* aren't getting married," Nancy answered patiently.

Disappointment drooped his smile. Her heart ached for her son, but the pain after Tom's death had been so great that nothing was going to ever make her risk that again.

"No?" A.J. was crushed.

Addie gave her brother a condescending look. "No, stupid. Just Mommy and Guy are getting married." She turned a confident face up to her mother, sure she had gotten it straight. "Right, Mommy?"

"Wrong, Addie."

Why had they suddenly gotten this bug into their heads? They'd never played matchmaker before. Why now? What was so special about the policeman next door? Aside from great eyes, terrific lips, a nice sense of humor... Nancy stopped cataloging his attributes abruptly. Whose side was she on, anyway?

She looked down at the children she had labeled her devilish duo for the enjoyment of her readers. "Look, he's a very nice man—"

"Super nice," Addie agreed enthusiastically.

"And his sister is nice, too," A.J. added shyly. He'd liked Demi. She was pretty, and she smelled good, too. Almost as nice as Mommy.

Nancy raised a brow. Puppy love, fueled by a large helping of chocolate cake, no doubt.

"Yes, I noticed how close you all became. Well, nice or not, I'm not marrying anyone. We're fine just the way we are, the three of us." She looked from one long face to the other. "Now, I don't want to hear any more about this, understand?"

"Understand," they chorused morosely.

No, they didn't, she thought, but she wasn't up to arguing with them. She had a deadline to beat and a column to write. Something good had to come out of this experience.

"Good. Now I have to get to work." Nancy turned to go to her room.

"If you married Guy, then Demi would be our aunt," A.J. called after her.

Nancy kept walking. "You already have aunts." She tossed the words over her shoulder. "Two of them, remember?"

A.J. followed in her wake, stopping just short of her bedroom. "But not with a dessert cart."

She didn't have to turn around to see his pout. She could hear it in his voice. Crossing to her computer, Nancy turned it on.

"All of us are deprived in one way or another, A.J." She looked over her shoulder. He was still standing in the doorway, a hangdog look on his face. *Not this time, little man. I'm wise to your tricks,* she thought. "Now, unless you also want to stop eating on a regular basis, I've got to get to work."

Instead of chasing A.J. away, her words flushed Addie out. Like a woman on a mission, she elbowed her twin out of the doorway and walked into the room. "But he's coming Saturday, right, Mommy? We heard you tell him to come over."

The computer asked for her password. Nancy typed in a hybrid of her children's names. The screen turned blank, then flashed the computer's specifications. "What you heard was Guy inviting himself over." She turned around in the chair, facing the doorway. "And I think it would be better all around if I told him not to come."

Addie and A.J. exchanged horrified looks. "Aw, Mommy!" they cried in unison.

But Nancy had already turned around again to face her computer. It was a signal for them to leave. This time, though, they hung back. Nancy could hear them shifting around behind her.

"Not another word about it," she warned.

First chance she got, she promised herself, she was going to tell Guy that she was canceling Saturday. Otherwise, she had a feeling the twins would be announcing her nuptials in the local newspaper before the day was out.

But the first chance Nancy got to tell Guy anything, she really wasn't up for conversation. Or dressed for it, either.

It was the following afternoon, and she had just stepped out of the shower. The towel she'd wrapped around herself was loosely secured at her breasts as she rubbed the excess moisture from her hair with another towel. She was definitely not expecting visitors.

Rounding the corner of the minuscule hall, she walked right into Guy, rapping her knee against the toolbox he was carrying.

The scream was purely reflexive.

Trying to compose herself and regain the normal timbre of her voice, she took a deep breath. It didn't really help.

"What are you doing here?" she cried.

He tried not to stare, he really did, but it wasn't easy. Not when the woman in front of him had a body that, soft, curvaceous and temptingly silky, practically begged for a man's hand.

Nor was it easy keeping the smile off his face.

Guy failed miserably at both endeavors.

With an effort, he raised his eyes to her face. For the moment, she looked too stunned to be angry.

That was a good sign, he supposed. At least it gave him a chance to explain.

"Um, the kids said you had a leak you wanted fixed."

"You remember, Mommy," Addie reminded her quickly. "The one in the bathroom." She pointed behind her mother. "In the shower. You said the drip was making you crazy and you wanted it fixed."

It took a minute for the words to register. Nancy vaguely remembered saying a few choice words after hanging up on the front office's maintenance department. The nasal woman answering phones had offered some flimsy excuse about putting her on a long list.

"Yes," she said pointedly, "but not while I was in it."

She had skin the color of whipped cream. He'd always had a great weakness for whipped cream.

"I'm sorry, when they asked me to take a look at it, I didn't realize that you were using it." The noise of the twin's chatter had blotted out the sound of the running water.

She supposed it wasn't his fault. Just as it wasn't his fault that her skin was tingling right now, warming rapidly under the heat of his gaze. These things just happened. But she wished they weren't happening to her.

Nancy felt her towel slipping and quickly secured it. "I'm the one who should apologize—"

"Not hardly," he murmured.

Hot. Now it was definitely getting hot in here, she thought. She tried to keep her mind on what she was saying.

"They had no right bothering you with this. I don't know what's come over them. The maintenance department is supposed to fix the leak." She fixed an accusing look on Addie.

"But Guy's right here," Addie insisted.

"That doesn't mean you can bother him." Nancy would have thrown up her hands, if she could. But that would only have led to more embarrassment. As it was, he probably thought she used her children to procure men. What else could he think? "They're really not usually like this. Dragging neighbors into the apartment is something new with them."

"I always like to get in on the ground floor of things." Fascinated, he watched the pink glow climb up her neck until it cleared a path to her cheek. "It's okay, really," he assured her. "I don't mind." He shifted the toolbox to his other hand, drawing her attention to it. "They made it sound like an emergency, so I came right over."

Addie and A.J. stood beside him now, innocent as lambs, hopeful as children on Christmas Eve. She wanted to be angry with them, she really did.

But she couldn't.

Nancy blew out a breath. "Well, it's nice to know that the cavalry is right next door if I ever need it, but this is really not necessary." What more could she say to get him to leave? she wondered desperately.

He wasn't leaving. She had to get into some clothes. She couldn't just continue standing here, talking to him, feeling as if any second, the terry cloth was going to evaporate because her skin temperature kept progressively rising.

"Hey, I'm here now, why not show me? Where the leak is, I mean." He was stumbling over his own tongue. Considering what she looked like, he was surprised he hadn't swallowed it by now. "I'm really pretty handy—at fixing leaks," he added after a beat, not wanting her to misunderstand.

Nancy was edging toward her room and her clothes. "I, um..."

Coming to the rescue, Addie took Guy by the hand. "I'll show you," she volunteered.

He went with her willingly. Another minute in Nancy's company and he was going to forget how to use anything in the toolbox.

A.J. looked up at his mother, beaming. Once she saw how nice it was to have Guy fix things, she'd marry him for sure.

"He's really handy," A.J. stressed.

She didn't doubt it, and she'd bet it wasn't the toolbox that bore witness to his best work. "A.J., what did I tell you?"

Wheat-colored eyebrows joined together in a squiggly line over the bridge of his small nose. "Not to talk to strangers, but he's not a stranger—"

That's for sure. "No, right now he's a little more familiar than I'd like." *Or want.* "But that's not what I'm talking about. I said that we were fine just the way we were and I didn't want you to bother Officer Tripopulous."

A.J. was quick to mount his own defense. "But Guy said it wasn't a bother."

Patient, she had to be patient. They meant well, they just didn't understand. "That's because he's only being nice, honey."

A.J. beamed. Mommy *did* understand. "See, Mommy, he *is* nice."

It was a losing battle. Nancy sighed, shaking her head. "What am I going to do with you and your sister, A.J.?"

He blinked, confused. "About what, Mommy?"

A complete losing battle. Maybe she could think better with her clothes on, instead of goose bumps. "Never mind, A.J. Never mind."

Nancy hurried into her room and changed as quickly as possible, before Addie could think of something Guy could fix in her bedroom. The girl was just too stubborn for her own good.

And hers, Nancy thought.

With a slash of lipstick representing makeup and a T-shirt and a pair of ragged cutoffs for clothes, Nancy hurried out again. She found Guy in the shower stall. The shower head was off, and he was replacing a washer. It occurred to her belatedly that he must have gone out and shut off the water while she was changing. The man was fast.

Too fast. She didn't want him working his way into her life any further.

No time like the present to put a stop to it. "About this Saturday night..." she began.

"Oh, yeah, Saturday." He glanced at her over his shoulder, then moved the shower head into position. "I'm really sorry, but I'm not going to be able to make it after all."

He said it so casually, she was left momentarily speechless.

He was canceling?

This was exactly what she wanted, without the anguish or discomfort of having to explain why she wanted it. So why did the news make her feel as if she'd just heard the announcement that Christmas had been abolished?

Nancy blinked, mystified at her reaction. "You're not?"

He worked the shower head back slowly, careful not to overtighten or strip the threads. "No, my sergeant wants some extra men working on a surveillance detail." Having been married to a policeman, he figured, she could appreciate this better than most women. "There've been a number of robberies in the county. Thieves breaking into computer warehouses, stealing the equipment and selling it on the black market. They've hit here twice in the last month, and the city fathers are not amused."

She'd seen so much of him out of uniform lately, she'd forgotten for a minute that he was a policeman. Forgotten, too, the reason for her initial resistance to him. She tried to picture him in a law-enforcement situation and felt her stomach tightening.

"Is it, um, dangerous?" Nancy flushed as soon as the words were out. "Stupid question." Of course it was dangerous. He was dealing with criminals.

Guy's smile put her at ease, or would have, if it weren't so damn sexy, she thought grudgingly.

"No, it's not a stupid question, and thanks for asking." He dropped his wrench into the toolbox and rummaged around for a smaller one. Guy shrugged. "It's not like walking into the middle of a gang war, but there's always an element of risk. Something as simple as stopping a speeding car is risky. You never know who's behind the wheel."

"Exactly." And it was just that worry that had haunted her every day Tom went to work. Until the worry became reality.

Leaning against the door jamb, Nancy watched Guy as he worked. She had a million things to do, the most important of which was going over her column—a very funny column, if she did say so herself. Yes, sir, there were a million reasons why she shouldn't be standing here like this, watching him like some schoolgirl, instead of the responsible mother of twins that she was.

But she couldn't get herself to move.

He had large, capable hands, she thought. For a moment, she wondered what those hands would feel like against her skin. Probably rough. They were undoubtedly callused.

The thought wasn't off-putting.

Nancy roused herself. Where were her chattering children when she needed them to run interference? Nancy ran the tip of her tongue over her lips. Guy chose that moment to look in her direction. Their eyes met and held. His were hypnotic. Nancy temporarily lost the use of her brain.

Her tongue engaged without it. "I don't know what the kids told you, but you really don't have to do that. Worse comes to worse, I can pay for a plumber."

"No need, I'm almost done. It's really very simple when you know what to do." She was going to protest again, he could see it in her eyes. "And it's my pleasure. I like working with my hands."

Guy squatted down to close the toolbox, then made the mistake of looking up, and almost shut the lid on his hand.

He wondered if she knew just how high some of those fringes on her shorts ran. Got a man started dreaming, he thought. "Helps work out the tension."

"Tension?"

"From the job." He spared her just one more long look. "And other things."

Why did that please her so much? Flirting, she

decided, clutching at the word in self-defense. Just harmless flirting. Nothing wrong in indulging in that. It was good for the soul.

As long as it stopped there.

She should go, Nancy told herself. The column was waiting. She shoved her hands into her pockets. "About Saturday—"

"Yes?" Guy didn't turn around. Skittish quarry always bolted at sudden movements.

Nancy stared at the back of his head. His hair curled so that it was hard to make out the ends. Would it curl that way around her fingers?

"Maybe we can reschedule."

She was more surprised than he was to hear the words coming out of her mouth. Now why had she gone and done that? She'd been safe a minute ago, and now she'd started the game all over again.

Guy rose to his feet, the job finished. His eyes touched hers. They were smiling. "I'd like that."

Nancy began backing out of the small room, determined to get to the safety of her keyboard. "Yes, me, too."

She wished she had been lying.

The Monday morning after spring recess ended ushered itself in with the usual chaos of suddenly remembered assignments that had been neglected and the hunt for mates to athletic shoes that had wantonly wandered off under their own power.

No matter how many speeches she made about

getting everything ready the night before, it always came down to this. A frenzied thirty minutes that involved shouting, searches, and lunches that were made on the fly.

Nancy was on her stomach, snaking her way under the raised sofa, where the hunt for A.J.'s lost shoe had finally ended, when she heard the doorbell.

She stretched, trying to snag a corner of the black toe with the tips of her fingers. How the hell had A.J. managed to fling his shoe back here?

The doorbell rang again. Who could possibly be at her door at this hour? she thought irritably.

"Ask who it is first," she called out as she heard two sets of feet eagerly running to the door. She vaguely heard Addie and A.J. vying for the privilege of being the first to open it.

"We know who it is," Addie called back.

"Who?" Nancy's question was obscured by a sneeze. It was amazing the amount of dust that could accumulate under a sofa. As usual, cleaning had worked its way down really low on her list of things to do. She should never have bought anything with carved legs, she thought grudgingly as she wiggled out into the open again.

"Me."

Surprised, Nancy turned abruptly and bumped her head against the coffee table. Not enough to hurt, just enough to embarrass her. The next moment, she felt strong arms encircling her, gently moving her onto the sofa.

Blinking, she cleared her head and looked up into eyes that reminded her of heaven.

Guy looked at her, concerned. From where he stood, she looked as if she'd hit her head pretty hard. He shouldn't have surprised her like that, but he had to admit, he'd gotten caught up in admiring the view as she crawled back out from under the sofa. She was wearing those cutoffs again.

"Are you all right?"

He was still holding her, she thought. She didn't want to like the feeling, but she did. "I am unless you're a hallucination."

He grinned. Belatedly he released her. "Then you're all right."

Nancy scrambled to compose herself, at least mentally, if not physically. She brushed off the edge of her shirt. She probably looked like a walking dust bunny, she thought disparagingly.

"At the risk of sounding like a broken record, what are you doing here?"

A.J. crowded in at her side. "He's our show-and-tell," he declared happily.

Maybe she *had* hit her head too hard. Nancy looked at her son. "He's what?"

"Our show-and-tell." It was Addie, not A.J., who answered. "We asked him and he said it was okay."

Nancy held up two hands, a signal for all talking to cease. She had to say this out loud to get it straight in her own mind.

"You're bringing Officer Tripopulous to school for show-and-tell?"

Blond heads bobbed up and down in unison. A.J. looked positively ecstatic about the prospect. "This is better than what Scottie Wilson brought. He just brought in his pet turtle," he added, in case Mommy had forgotten he'd told her that. That had been the day he came home and asked for a pet turtle himself. He'd gotten shot down by Mommy and Addie, who didn't like turtles. Addie had asked for a dumb old cat, and Mommy had said, "We'll see," which meant no, but that was okay, 'cause he didn't like cats. He liked turtles.

Guy hadn't heard this part of the story. "Nice to know where I fit in in the pecking order."

"Officer Tripopulous isn't a pet," Nancy pointed out. *And he's not yours to show off,* she thought. This really was getting way out of hand.

"No, but he's a neighbor," Addie said, with a diplomacy that temporarily left Nancy speechless. "And Teacher said we can bring in anything we like as long as it won't mess up the classroom or run away."

"I'm housebroken," Guy assured Nancy with an engaging grin.

She let out a breath. "I'm sure you are." Well, if he didn't mind, who was she to stand in the way?

Nancy got up from the sofa and handed A.J. his shoe. It was getting late. "All right, get your things together and I'll drive you to school."

Guy placed a restraining hand on her wrist. Nancy tried to stop the tingling sensation from traveling up her arm, clear to her scalp. She might as well have been trying to turn the wind by blowing at it, for all the good it did.

"Why don't I drive them? Since I have to go in anyway," Guy added. "There's no sense in both of us driving. Just trying to get some of the excess traffic off the road," he said in response to the quizzical look on her face. "And this'll give you a chance to get an extra cup of coffee before you start to work."

She was way ahead in that department. "One more cup of coffee and they're liable to have to pry me off the ceiling."

"Then don't let them get started without me."

Why the hell did that sound so sexy?

To Nancy's amazement, Addie and A.J. presented themselves to Guy within two minutes, completely ready to leave. None of the wild, last-minute running around that she habitually encountered. Getting them off to school was like trying to round up an army of floppy-eared, large-pawed puppies. You no sooner had one ready than another broke free. Someone was always forgetting something. On the average, it took them five tries to finally make it out of the carport.

Guy made it in one smooth execution.

The man definitely performed magic, Nancy

thought with a sigh as she watched Guy drive away with her children.

And on more than just the twins, she added ruefully.

But, magic or not, she knew what the rules were. She'd set them down for herself four years ago. And she meant to abide by them. Even if it wasn't easy.

She heard him when he pulled in an hour later. It was hard not to. Especially since she'd been waiting for him to return. The desk in her bedroom faced the side where Guy parked his car. With the window open, it seemed rude not to say anything when he passed.

She was making excuses to herself. What was worse, she knew it.

He saw her sitting there and wondered if she was waiting for him. The answer was probably no, but he liked to think that there was a chance that she might be.

Nancy looked up, as if surprised to see him approach. She pushed the curtain back farther, away from the window. "So, how did it go?"

He'd been a hit. So much so that the acting principal had asked him to address a special assembly. Guy had delivered an impromptu talk. Addie and A.J. had sat right up front, beaming and feeling very pleased with themselves.

"Pretty well, I think." He played it down. "I'm beginning to have new respect for Bob and Gary."

She cocked her head. "Bob and Gary?"

"The two officers who make the rounds on the elementary school circuit. They hold assemblies, interact with the kids, answer any questions," he explained. "It's the police department's way of making friends with kids while they're still young. Hopefully, we discourage any behavioral problems before they occur."

He leaned a shoulder against the wall, wishing he had the time to get himself invited in.

"They tell kids to avoid gangs, and how bad drugs are for them. The usual. In a place like Bedford, it's not too hard." He smiled at his own naiveté. "Or so I thought. But boy, they can sure be a handful."

She liked the fact that it didn't threaten his masculinity to admit to being overwhelmed. "Do I detect a little droop in those wings?"

He wasn't following her. "Wings?"

She nodded. "Well, the way you were putting up with the twins, I was beginning to think you had the patience of a saint, or an angel."

He laughed. Now there was a image. "Talk to Demi about that." He straightened. "Well, I'd better get going. I just stopped to get some papers. I'm due at the precinct in fifteen minutes. I only signed out for half a day."

"You used your own time off to do this?"

He shrugged it off. "Hey, it beats paperwork."

The words on her computer screen had vanished,

replaced by spaceships that were flying into one another. She moved back from the window. "Speaking of which, I'd better get back to work myself. Thanks again."

"Don't mention it." He winked at her, then left, saying something about seeing her later.

Nancy stared at the screen, unable to make sense of anything she read. Instead, she kept seeing a very sexy wink and wondering exactly when "later" meant.

This was not a good sign.

6

Now what do I do?

Nancy worked her lower lip in frustration as she hung up the telephone. She'd been trying to get through to Summer on the teenager's personal line for the past twenty minutes. Each time the receiver was picked up, thundering noise that passed for music echoed in the background as Summer's prerecorded voice instructed her to "Like, leave a message when it, you know, beeps."

Nancy had already left one message, and she was sorely tempted to leave a second, more terse one. But that would be just her annoyance talking, and it wouldn't be fair to take it out on anyone.

Summer was definitely not her first choice, but she'd been practically her last hope.

What was she supposed to do now?

Nancy debated calling Albert back to try to postpone the meeting, but her editor had sounded adamant about seeing her this afternoon. He'd given her no indication what this was about, and she'd known better than to ask. Albert had his own way of doing things, and she needed this job. Where else could she get paid for putting her opinions down in seven hundred and fifty words, give or take, and work out of the house so she was available for her kids whenever they needed her?

No, the job was a godsend, even if Albert wasn't at times.

So what was she going to do with the twins?

A.J. looked up from the book he had been laboring over. He and Addie were sitting on opposite ends of the kitchen table, papers, books, pencils and snacks covering the space between them. It was homework time, and A.J. and his sister would rather be anywhere else in the world but here.

He saw the frown on his mother's face as she hung up again. This time, Mommy had let the receiver drop down pretty hard. She didn't usually lose her temper. Mommy was upset.

"What's the matter, Mommy?"

Nancy dragged an impatient hand through her hair. It fell back into her eyes. Nothing, it seemed, was going right today.

"Hmm? Oh, nothing, honey." She gave the telephone a black look. "I just can't seem to reach Summer."

"Summer?" Addie made a face, as if she'd just swallowed dirt. "How come you're calling her?"

Not to be outdone, A.J. raised his voice. "Yeah, how come?"

She knew she'd promised them that Summer was

history, but she was desperate. None of the other sitters she usually fell back on were available, either. Nancy glanced at her watch. She was going to have to get going soon. Albert's pet peeve was being kept waiting. He might already be in a black mood, and she didn't want to push it.

"My editor wants me to come in for a meeting, and I can't take you with me."

Addie drew herself up at the table, gaining perhaps an inch, perhaps less. "I can watch A.J. I'm big."

Thin shoulders became ramrod-straight. "I'm big, too."

They could always make her smile. "Yeah, and together you add up to big trouble."

Nancy looked at the long faces that greeted her words. They wanted so much to hurry up and be grown. Little did they realize that their mother would give anything just to be in their shoes. Worrying about finishing your homework in time to watch TV instead of being concerned about your job would be wonderful right about now.

She crossed to the table. "I know you want to be all grown up, and for me, you are." So, she lied— at least it made them happy, she thought. "But it's against the law to leave kids your age by themselves for a long time. You don't want me to go to jail, do you?"

A.J. shook his head.

Addie, on the other hand, was inspired. Jails had

policemen, and so did they. At least one. "Hey, why don't we ask—?"

Nancy was one step ahead of her. Addie just didn't give it a rest, did she?

"No. Besides, he's probably not home." She didn't keep track of his work hours, but she assumed they fit into the usual eight-to-five domain somewhere.

A.J. caught on, and was quick to add in his two cents. "Yes, he is." It would be nice, he thought, having Guy over, pretending that they were with their daddy, watching TV. He could hardly wait. "I hear music coming from inside." A.J. pointed in the general direction of Guy's apartment. "He likes the loud stuff."

A.J. had better ears than she did, Nancy thought. So why was it, she wondered, bemused, that he hardly ever heard her when she called him? "We can't impose."

Addie didn't like it when Mommy used words she didn't know. "What's impose?"

Nancy put it in terms they could understand. "Make a pest of ourselves."

Like a junkyard dog, Addie refused to give up. "But he likes us."

She didn't need this. Nancy sighed. "It's like candy, honey. Too much makes you sick."

"I won't make him sick, I promise." A.J. held up his left hand, the way he'd seen a witness on TV do when he was sworn in by a judge. Belatedly he switched hands, remembering that it was right, not left.

Nancy shook her head and started paging through her worn address book. There had to be somebody she could call. "Let me see who else I can find."

But she couldn't find anyone. Everyone she called was either out or busy. There was no one who could drop everything on a Thursday afternoon to stay with her children.

She was beginning to feel as if it were a plot. And time was really running short. Albert wanted her there by four-thirty. If she caught all the lights, she could make it. Just.

Surrendering, Nancy threw up her hands. "All right, I guess, if he doesn't mind—"

She didn't have to say anything else. Addie was on her feet and out of the apartment like a shot. Not bothering to close the door behind her, she ran to Guy's apartment across the way and began knocking insistently.

When Guy opened the door on the third knock, Addie didn't give him a chance to even say hello. Instead, she hooked her fingers around his and began dragging him toward her apartment.

"Mommy *really needs* you," she declared breathlessly, secretly pleased that she could be the one to tell him this.

Adrenaline pumped immediately. For a moment, he forgot that this was the child who had brought him a ransom note. If Nancy had sent her for him, after a week of practically going into hiding, something had to be wrong.

But as he crossed the threshold to the twins' apartment, suspicion reared its head. Was he being duped again? Nancy didn't exactly look like a lady who had been sending up distress signals. As a matter of fact, she looked uncomfortable about seeing him here.

He hated being made a fool of, even if he did like the kids. Guy crossed his arms as he looked at Nancy. "Did you send for me?"

Nancy felt awkward. She didn't want him to feel that he was being summoned. "Not in so many words."

Grown-ups talked too slow. Addie took matters back into her hands.

"She needs you," Addie insisted. "Nobody can stay with us, and she's gotta go talk to Albert."

A dark, sculpted brow cocked over darkening eyes. It was almost hard to tell that they were even green. "Albert?"

"My editor," Nancy explained, then turned to look at her daughter. "Mr. Dawson." Addie was much too relaxed and familiar when it came to adults. But teaching her a little respect and restraint was low on Nancy's priority list right now, nudged aside by the need to keep her job. She looked at Guy, hoping he could help her out. "And I am in kind of a jam. I haven't really found a regular sitter for the twins yet and no one seems to be available today.''

When she paused for breath, eyeing him nervously, he asked, ''Is this where I'm supposed to say I can?''

There was distance between them. It made the request even more awkward. ''Only if you're free.''

''Well, I am,'' he allowed, studying her. He was still trying to figure her out. His male friends told him this kind of thing could take years—if it ever came about. ''I just didn't want to overstep any boundary lines you might have drawn.''

She deserved that, she thought. Frightened by the fact that something within her had been steadily defrosting in the heat generated by her response to Guy, she'd gone out of her way to avoid him. When their paths did cross, she'd been distantly polite. He'd gotten the message, and though she had to admit it bothered her that he received it so well, she knew it was for the best.

Whose best was a matter up for discussion at some future date, not now.

She was desperate, and he was all she had to work with. She didn't have time to explain herself or what she was feeling. Or what she was trying not to feel.

''I'll pay you,'' she offered. It seemed only fair. She would have paid anyone else.

He'd already decided to help out, anyway. ''Good, I'll think of a price.''

His answer made the edginess return. "It's usually four dollars an hour."

Dark blue eyes met green. Just a hint of a smile entered them. "I wasn't thinking about money."

Oh, God, that strange sensation was back. The one that made her stomach feel as if a tsunami were imminent. "Maybe this isn't—"

She was going to ruin everything, Addie thought in exasperation.

"Mommy, don't you have to go?" Addie began tugging her toward the door.

Yes, she did. But not barefoot. "At least let me get my shoes," Nancy protested. Reluctantly, Addie let go of her arm. God, but they were eager to get her out of the apartment.

"Here, Mommy, here they are." A.J. held up an athletic shoe in each hand. The colors were only vaguely similar.

Nancy smiled. Her little husband-in-training, she thought. A.J. couldn't find his nose if he looked in the mirror. The shoes he was holding up were not mates. Each belonged to a different pair.

But he meant well.

"Not those, sweetie. I'll be right back," she promised, disappearing into her room.

When she returned two minutes later, she had shoes on her feet and a briefcase in her hand. And a running list of instructions on her tongue.

Cornering Guy, she began issuing them. "All right now, they have to do their homework before they can watch any TV,'' she warned as two sets of small hands were pushing her out the door.

Before she could get any farther down her list of instructions, she found herself on the other side of the front door.

"I'll hold down the fort," Guy promised, flanked by the twins.

Almost against her will, she noted that they made a nice picture, framed in the doorway like that. But she had an uneasy feeling that the fort might be burned down by the time she returned.

No time to worry about that now, she reminded herself. She had an editor to placate. And maybe a job to save.

It was hard to walk out when your editor was singing your praises, but she should have excused herself an hour ago, Nancy thought, glancing at the clock on the dashboard. Three hours. Oh, God, she'd left Guy with the twins for three hours. Anything could have happened in that amount of time.

Reaching for her portable phone, she punched in her home number. The annoying throb of a busy signal greeted her ear. Nancy frowned.

Why was it busy? She had call waiting. One of the twins must have knocked the receiver off its cradle. Sighing, she pressed the red button, ending the call.

It took very little for her to visualize the state her apartment would be in after three hours of unrestrained twins. Never neat, it probably looked like the aftermath of a war. Guy was undoubtedly at his wit's end. Those computer thieves he was on the trail of were probably looking pretty good to him right about now.

She knew from experience that the twins could stay on their good behavior for only so long, and they had already exceeded their limit.

Sooner or later, their true colors would show. And unfortunately, they matched those flying over a pirate's vessel.

She started to grin.

Again.

It was hard to allow anxiety to rise to the surface right now. Not when she felt so good.

Syndicated.

Such a little word, such a great feeling. She rolled it over on her tongue. *Syndicated.* Her. Who would have ever thought—?

But it was true. Albert had no sense of humor, so she knew it wasn't a joke. There were times when she'd despaired of ever making him smile, but it didn't matter. She didn't have to make Albert smile. All she had to do was sell papers, and judging by the letters that were coming in about her column, she was.

Her column was going national. People in Peoria and Upper Sandusky were going to take tiny peeks into her life over their breakfast each morning.

Or their parakeets were, looking at it on the bottom of their cages.

Didn't matter. She was syndicated.

Yes!

She felt as if she could bend steel in her bare hands if asked to.

Probably so could Guy, she thought, but for him it would be out of frustration, not from a euphoric high. Three hours of unadulterated Addie and A.J. could make strong men cry. And he was a strong man.

Nancy remembered the way his arms had felt around her when he picked her up from the floor the day he went in as the twins' show-and-tell project.

A very strong man.

She felt her breath getting caught in her throat and told herself she was going too fast. It was just the wind, hitting her face, snatching her breath away. Pressing the control button, she raised the window on the driver's side. Just as she had raised the walls around herself, she thought. Keeping him out.

And trapping herself in.

She felt too good to be having any sad thoughts, and she forced them away. She had kids to get to, and a policeman to rescue.

Going a little faster than she knew she should, Nancy reached home in a matter of minutes.

Jamming her key into the lock, she twisted it open and entered talking. "Hi, sorry I'm late," she called out to Guy. "Hope you didn't have too much—trouble?"

She stopped abruptly and looked around.

Was this her apartment?

It couldn't be. She'd entered the Twilight Zone, she thought, stunned.

"It's neat," she whispered.

"Yes, it is," Addie proudly announced, running up to greet her.

"We cleaned up for you, Mommy," A.J. added needlessly, attaching himself to her other side. Then, because he never wanted to take credit when it wasn't his, he told her, "Guy thought it was a good idea."

How had they managed this? There wasn't a single thing out of place. Except for the dust. That was missing.

Nancy walked slowly around, thinking that any second, all of this was going to disappear. She was having just too good an afternoon and evening for it to be true.

"It's a fabulous idea," she agreed, regaining her normal voice. "It just never seemed to fly when I said it." The books were gone from the table. She might have known. "But you should have done your homework instead." She knew she should have called and checked on them early. Now she was going to be up all night with them, struggling with assignments.

"We did," Addie said.

This was a little too hard to believe. Were there open pods lying around somewhere like in *The Body Snatchers?* "All of it?"

A.J.'s head bobbed like a bouncing handball. "Guy helped me make up sentences."

"And he even went on the Internet to get a history answer for me," Addie interjected.

That would explain the busy signal. Nancy fisted her hand on her hips as she looked down into the proud, shining faces. "All right, who are you and what have you done with my children?"

"We are your children, Mommy," A.J. cried, confused. "Really."

She hugged him, laughing, then drew Addie to her, as well. "I know you are, honey. I'm just surprised, that's all."

Actually, "surprised" was putting it mildly. "State of shock" only began to approximate her reaction.

Nancy looked over their heads at Guy. "I guess we'll have to add miracle worker to your growing list of credits."

The grin was not slow in coming. Neither was her reaction to it. Her resistance was definitely on the downswing. "Do I have a growing list of credits?"

There was no point in denying it. She'd never done coy well.

"Yeah, you do." She disentangled herself from her children. "Okay, it's late and I have great news, but first, let me get dinner going."

A.J. didn't give her a chance to get to the refrigerator. He tugged on her sleeve. "You don't hafta get it going. It's already gone, Mommy."

She was trying to think of what she had available that could be quickly converted into a meal. "What are you talking about?"

Addie flanked her other side, blocking any access to the refrigerator. "Guy made us dinner."

She digested this newest piece of information. "You mean takeout."

"No, put-in." A.J. rubbed his stomach and licked his lips simultaneously. "Right here. It tastes as good as what we had before. You know, when he took us out."

Nancy's brain felt as if it were still stuck in first gear. She turned around to look at Guy. "You cooked dinner?" Most men's idea of making dinner was opening the box the pizza came in and taking out the slices.

His expression answered her question. Guy shrugged. "Hey, you can't live two-thirds of your life over a restaurant without picking up a few things." He gently steered her toward the kitchen table. Dinner was in a covered casserole dish in the oven. "We didn't know when you'd be back, so we kept it warm for you."

She liked the way he said "we," and so did the twins. She could see it in their faces.

"Good with kids, plumbing and stoves." Not to

mention gorgeous, she added silently. Nancy looked at him suspiciously. "Why aren't you married?"

And where had he heard that before? He grinned in response. "My mother and grandmother ask the same question."

The teasing note left her voice. "What do you tell them?" The next moment, she had the oddest feeling that his smile meant business.

"That I hadn't found the right person."

She noticed he used the past tense, but that might have just been an accident. Accident or not, she wasn't going to let herself dwell on it. She didn't want to spoil the high she was on.

Or endanger it.

Guy opened the cupboard next to the sink and took out a dinner plate and a glass. "Hungry?"

He knew his way around her apartment as well as she did, Nancy thought. As if he'd always been here, always a part of this scene.

Something sad and distant stirred within her. Reaching out.

Nancy nodded. "Yes."

He expected nothing less. He'd put everything he had into making dinner, utilizing ingredients from his own kitchen when he couldn't find them in hers. When a man cooked for a woman, it should involve his heart and not her purse. It was something his grandmother had once whispered to him when his grandfather wasn't listening. He'd found out later that his grandfather had cooked for his grandmother when he was courting her. The old man vehemently denied it when asked, but Guy knew better. Grandmother had never lied to him.

"A.J.," he said, looking over his shoulder at the boy, "get your mother a can of soda out of the refrigerator."

Guy placed a casserole dish Nancy didn't recognize in the middle of the table and began to spoon out a portion on her plate. The aroma was delicious. And familiar.

"You made shepherd's pie." She looked at him, astounded. "I don't have potatoes."

"I do."

Out of the corner of her eye, she saw A.J. place the soda can on the table. Addie was smoothing out a paper napkin for her. How *did* he do it?

Black magic. That had to be the answer, she decided. Nothing else would have worked.

They sat down in a semicircle around her, obviously content just to watch her eat. She raised her fork, then stopped, looking at the three of them one by one. Her gaze rested on Guy.

"This is a dream, right?"

Yes, she was that, he thought. And he'd made up his mind that he wasn't going to let her get away just because she had some stubborn notion that this wasn't right. He was going to make her see that it was.

"If it is, we're both having it."

She begged to differ. "I don't know about that.

Your apartment didn't just get cleaned, your children didn't just do their homework without being threatened, and you didn't just get your column syndicated."

"No," he agreed, "but you didn't just get smiled at the way I did."

It was hard not to smile, when joy insisted on bursting out of every pore. "Oh?"

"Yeah, right from the heart, straight to the eyes." Eyes that haunted a man's dreams at night, he thought. Eyes that belonged to a woman he wanted to see beside him when he woke in the morning.

Every morning.

Guy roused himself. "Syndicated, huh?"

"Yes." A few minutes ago, she'd felt as if that were the best thing that could have happened to her and the twins. Now she wasn't so sure.

What she was sure of, though, was that she felt as giddy as a little girl. And getting the column syndicated didn't have all that much to do with it.

7

They weren't her kids.

Nancy was convinced of it. Oh, they looked just like Addie and A.J., all right, but these little polite clones just weren't her kids.

The twins had never been really bad, but they could have easily taught Mischief 101 without resorting to any written notes or needing to bone up on the subject. They had it down cold.

Yet tonight, Addie and A.J. had done their homework, helped clean up the apartment and cleared away her dishes when she finished eating, and were now volunteering to go to bed at what was, for them, the unheard-of hour of eight-thirty.

Volunteering.

That just about took her breath away. It usually took threats of being eternally grounded and permanently separated from beloved Saturday-morning cartoons and cherished stuffed animals to achieve what was now happening seemingly on its own. Nancy couldn't remember when bedtime hadn't been a power struggle littered with pleas for "five more minutes" and frantic attempts at bartering for grace periods.

She looked at Guy skeptically after A.J. and Addie trooped into their room like two well-behaved, brave little soldiers. "Tell me, if I look beneath the sofa cushions in the living room, will I find a tranquilizer gun and darts stuffed under there?"

He laughed at the image. The twins had been the model of politeness and obedience—and pretty damn eager to leave the two of them alone. He was crazy about them.

Guy shrugged innocently in answer to her question. "Hey, I specialize in crowd control, and your two—"

"Can qualify as a crowd any day, yes, I've been told that." Her mouth curved in a fond smile. Distance made difficult scenes that had exasperated her at the time seem amusing now. "Often. Usually by saleswomen and waitresses."

She looked up at him, forgetting for a moment to be afraid of this feeling that insisted on sizzling through her. Forgetting to keep her guard up. Her children liked this man, and he obviously liked them. That earned him a special place in her heart.

Although, she warned herself, that didn't mean that he had any right to the rest of it. She damn well knew the danger in that. "They really took to you."

He took the dish she'd removed from the dishwasher from her hands and placed it into the cupboard. "What can I say? Short people like me."

He was behaving like a husband. Better than a husband. She had to remember that he wasn't. And wouldn't be—at least not hers.

Nancy deliberately turned away as she took two glasses out of the rack, afraid he'd read too much in her eyes. "Tall people, too, I'd be willing to guess."

His hands touched hers as he reached for the glasses. "Is there a hidden message there?"

No, no contact. Contact only made things worse. It made her forget that she could do without being held and kissed. That she was just fine on her own.

Alone.

Nancy dropped her hands to her sides. She could put the rest of the dishes away later. "I'd better go tuck them in."

"Said she, evasively," Guy called after her.

She paused long enough to look at him over her shoulder. "Very funny. Maybe you should write a column of your own."

"Maybe."

Guy watched as she disappeared into the twins' bedroom. No doubt about it, he thought, grinning to himself, the view was inspiring.

Nancy closed the door behind her quietly. The scene before her could have come right out of one of the illustrated storybooks she read to them at bedtime. A.J. and Addie were both nestled in their bunk beds, curled up and looking like angels.

They didn't fool her for a minute.

"All right, you two, I'm on to you. You're not asleep. It's only been ten minutes since you came in here."

Picking the one she knew would break first, Nancy squatted down beside the lower bunk and fixed her son with a steady gaze.

A.J. opened one eye, then the other. He pressed his lips together to keep back a giggle. They could never fool Mommy, but it was fun to try. "We were almost asleep," he told her.

Nancy splayed a hand over her chest, exhibiting the proper amount of shock and hurt. "Before I could tuck you in and kiss you good-night? For shame."

She proceeded to do both, first with Addie, who always took longer to settle down, then with A.J.

The little boy snuggled against her and whispered, "How's it going?"

Nancy bit her lower lip to keep from laughing. He sounded just like a little old man when he asked that. Her little old man.

"It's going fine, but that doesn't mean you're supposed to get your hopes up." She rose to her feet and looked first at one, then the other. "Remember our agreement."

"We remember," the twins chorused.

Yeah, right. She knew better than to think that they weren't plotting against her behind those big, innocent eyes of theirs. After all, they were her kids, and she'd never been known to give up when it came to anything she wanted.

And apparently they wanted to have a tongue twister for a last name.

Sorry, guys, not this time. Mommy's got to think of Mommy once in a while.

"Glad we have an understanding," she said solemnly, as if she actually believed that they meant what they said. "Now go to sleep, tomorrow's a school day." She was at the door, about to leave, when she turned around. "Oh, and the apartment looks really great. See that you keep it that way."

Hey, she thought, it was worth a shot.

Her son obviously was intent on using the ammunition she'd given him, but not in a way she would have guessed. He popped up in his bunk like toast. "Okay, but we need Guy to help us."

Addie hung off the top bunk like a daredevil aerialist. "Yeah, Guy can really clean."

Nice try, but it ain't gonna work. "Guess it's just going to have to get messy again," Nancy told them with a dramatic sigh. "Now get back up, Addie, before you fall off."

Laughing under her breath, Nancy eased the door closed behind her.

And bumped right into Guy.

She stifled a gasp of surprise, not just at the unexpected sight of him, but at the unexpected feel of him, as well. His arms had encircled her instinctively to forestall a collision. And to bring about something else in its place.

Like a leg that had inadvertently fallen asleep, only to be pressed into use suddenly, she felt pins and needles moving all along her body. Ignoring the tingling sensation was impossible. Enjoying it didn't seem right.

"They heard that sigh all the way down to San Diego." Guy smiled into her eyes, waiting a beat before releasing her. A man had to find small pleasures somewhere. "Anything wrong?"

Yeah, you're standing too close and I like it. She shook her head, regaining composure she hoped he hadn't noticed she'd lost. "Just my kids trying to sell me on something."

He cocked a brow, interested. "What?"

She could have lied. Easily. He'd never know the difference. But she didn't. "You."

Guy grinned. "You know, maybe they're on to something. You know what they say—out of the mouths of babes…"

He was outmatched, she thought. She could give him cliché for cliché, if that was what he wanted. "They also say once burnt, twice leery."

Unfazed, Guy asked, "How about nothing ventured, nothing gained?"

"Look before you leap," she countered.

"Okay, a stitch in time saves nine." His eyes danced with amusement.

He'd lost her. "I'll bite. What's that supposed to mean?"

"Maybe," he said, toying with the ends of her hair, somehow managing to send delicious currents of electricity up along her neck, "it means that if you take advantage of what's right out in front of you, you won't wind up alone and regretting it somewhere down the line."

Now that was really reaching. "No, it means do something now when the problem is small, before you wind up having to do twice as much work later because you've let it go."

He shrugged. "Close enough."

"Not hardly." The way she saw it, if she took a "stitch" now, by picking up the guard that she was allowing to drop, she wouldn't have to do a whole lot of damage control with her heart later. Any way she looked at it, she just couldn't let her feelings go.

Maybe what she needed was to talk, rather than to avoid.

But it wasn't easy.

Feeling her way around, she started slowly. "Guy, it's not that I don't like you, or appreciate everything you've done and how patient you've been with the twins, but this just can't go anywhere."

It wasn't eloquent, she thought, but at least it was to the point. It wasn't fair to let him think that, just because the twins were in his corner, this was going to turn into something more permanent.

He looked into her eyes and found the answers to questions he wouldn't put to her aloud just yet. "And that's because...?"

She sighed. He really wasn't making this easy on her. That gave him a lot in common with her kids.

"Because I have my commitments already mapped out. To my children," she enumerated. "To my work. And to Tom. There isn't room for anything else."

But Tom was dead, and she wasn't. She was very much alive. Guy took her hands in his, studying her face. "How about you?"

"Me?" She didn't understand. She was telling him about herself, about her commitments. Wasn't he paying attention?

"You," he repeated softly. "Isn't there room in there for your feelings?"

"I told you, they're already taken up."

No, they weren't. She wouldn't have responded to him the way she had when he kissed her if that was true. "I'm afraid I'm not as convinced about that as you are. The attraction between us is growing, Nancy. I can feel it."

She drew her hands away from him. It wasn't as easy drawing her feelings away. But he didn't have to know that. "I..."

He wanted her to hear him out. And to think about what he said. "You might not want to admit it, but you need someone, Nancy. We all do. Someone to talk to, someone to lean on once in a while. Someone to hold your hand and say nothing at all if the moment calls for it.''

She moved away from him. But there was nowhere to go. Everything seemed to be coming back in a circle. "Well, then, that can't be me. I've never been known not to talk.''

He laughed. ''Adjustments can be made to fit the case.'' And then he grew serious, because feelings were serious things. "I know I need someone.'' He ran his hand through her hair. It rained through his fingers like golden rays. "Someone with long, silky blond hair.'' His thumb lightly brushed along the outline of her lips. Heat flared where he touched. "Someone with a mouth made for kissing and eyes as blue as cornflowers. Someone who'll be there when I reach out for her.''

She was afraid, he thought, really afraid. He did his best to set her at ease.

"My grandfather has been married to my grandmother for over fifty-one years. My parents will be married thirty this September. The Tripopulous men mate for life.'' He grinned. "Kind of like eagles. And puffins.'' The smile that rose to her lips gave him hope. "How about it, Nancy? Why don't you just give 'us' a try? If it doesn't work out, there's a money-back guarantee.''

Mate for life. Those were his words. But what if that life stopped? What if it was cut short? It was better not to love than to hurt again.

She shook her head. "I—I can't.''

He swept her hair from her face, framing it with his large, gentle hands. For a long moment, he just stood there and looked at her. "Nancy, you're going to have to understand something."

"What?" She wanted to sound flippant, blasé, anything to turn him off. But it was hard to do when her voice was so hoarse.

"Just because I arrived at the party late doesn't mean that I don't want to take you home after the dance is over."

Excitement and fear entwined in her soul, tearing her apart. She wanted. Wanted so badly. And knew that she couldn't.

Her torment was there in her eyes for him to see. The pain she'd suffered, the longing that had been aroused. He wouldn't press her any more, not tonight. He could wait.

"I have to get going," he told her. "I'm on the night shift this week."

She felt as if she'd just gotten a call from the governor a moment before the switch was thrown. Nancy let out a long, measured breath as she followed him to the front door. "Well, thanks again."

He stopped, his hand on the doorknob. "I don't want your thanks, Nancy."

If she'd never married Tom, things might have been different between her and Guy. But she had, and it had changed the way she looked at everything. "I can't give you what you want."

The smile was soft, patient. "Oh, we'll see.

Meanwhile, I've got to go." He began to open the door, then paused. "But before I leave, I just want to give you something else to think about."

More guilt—just what she needed. Nancy braced herself. "What?"

He turned around. "This."

A five-year-old could have seen it coming.

But a five-year-old wouldn't have had her mind clouded with juxtaposed feelings. A five-year-old wouldn't have had the trauma of wanting desperately to resist being put in the position of being hurt again. Of wanting never again to feel the kind of pain that cut you in two and left you bleeding.

So he took her completely by surprise when his mouth came down on hers, not gently, like a dove landing on a thin perch, but like a hawk, swooping down on something that had caught his eye. Snatching it away.

Just as Guy snatched her breath away. With absolutely no effort at all.

She fell into the kiss, head over heels, end over end, with nothing to hold on to, nothing to anchor herself with. One minute she was there, the next minute she was gone, swallowed up by an abyss as his firm lips worked to seal her doom.

And as his tongue, lightly outlining her lips, stole away her will to resist.

She was going to melt right here, Nancy thought, and then evaporate without a trace. No one would even know she'd ever existed.

Why was it, when he was trying his best to undermine her resolve, that he succeeded in getting himself so totally captured by the opposition? How could a woman with two children possess innocence, and then be so damn sensual on top of it?

It was a paradox, a quandary.

Whatever it was called, it amounted to his utter undoing.

A weaker man would probably have fallen to his knees and begged. A weaker man would certainly have succumbed to the desire and passion thundering through him, demanding release, and tried his best to push the advantage he tasted in her kiss. A weaker man would have found a way to get himself into her bed.

But, weak or strong, Guy wasn't out for the short tumble or a finite, tempestuous affair. What he wanted was to be there for the long haul. And it wouldn't be attainable if he took unfair advantage.

Wasn't very damn fair, her making him feel as if he had scrambled eggs for brains, either, but that was the way things were right now. He was damn well going to have to make the best of it.

Bracing himself, working to steady breathing that had all but become ragged, Guy drew away from her. He was surprised, and pleased, when his knees actually functioned.

"Think on that when I'm gone."

And then he was.

Think? He expected her to think? With what?

He'd fried her brain cells to a crisp, she thought grudgingly. She would probably never be able to do long division again.

Nancy leaned against the front door and stayed there, knowing that at the moment, making the long trip to the sofa was completely out of the question.

And as she remained pressed against the cool surface, she wondered if he had made his way through a legion of girls and women to learn how to kiss that way, or if it was something he'd just been born with.

Either way, it was a national treasure.

She was losing her battle, and she knew it.

In the two weeks since Guy performed the Miracle of the Docile Twins, Nancy had found herself the center of a conspiracy every time she turned around. A.J. and Addie were on one side, Guy was on the other, and the sides were closing in on her, making her feel that life was incomplete without the unit they formed.

She wasn't even really sure just how it had all come about. A month ago, she'd been a single mother, struggling to raise her two children and writing about the foibles all that entailed. Now she was part of an unspoken set.

They hadn't discussed anything any further than that fried parting at the door the night he'd left for work, but somehow, some way, she must have taken another step toward a relationship, because it certainly felt as if she were in one.

She wanted it.

And she didn't.

At a time and place in her life where she'd been certain she would finally be settled, she was in the middle of a complete emotional revolution. Whenever she tried to talk sense into herself, to resist giving in to feelings that were progressively getting deeper and stronger, she failed miserably.

The truth was that she liked being with him. Liked seeing the twins with him. Guy was funny, and kind, and he could cook.

The man was damn near perfect.

Except that he was a cop.

But cop or not, Nancy found herself listening for his car, for the sound of his whistle as he walked up the path to his door in the afternoon. Listening for it, and looking forward to seeing him again.

Logically, she knew she was on emotional quicksand, but the more she resisted, or tried to, the deeper she sank into it.

Right about now, she was hip-deep in mud and sinking fast.

"Don't grow up," she advised suddenly, looking up from her notepad at A.J.

A.J. and Addie were both on their stomachs in front of the TV, their hands wrapped around control pads wired to the electronic game they were playing. On the screen, a squat little man with a droopy black mustache that was almost as long as he was tall suddenly froze in midleap, thanks to the pause button.

A.J. wiggled into a sitting position as he looked at his mother. "Why not?"

She couldn't help glancing at the window that faced Guy's door. "Because it's just too complicated when you do."

A.J. didn't like it when Mommy looked like that. It made his tummy feel all funny, like someone was squeezing it. "Are you sad, Mommy? We did our homework."

She should be ashamed of herself. She had her kids—what more could she ask for?

More, a tiny voice whispered. So much more.

"Yes, I know you did," she told A.J. "And I'm not sad."

Addie, who'd been listening silently up to now, was unconvinced. "Your eyes are sad. Wait," Addie said, shoving her control pad at A.J., springing to her feet. "I'll go get Guy. He'll make you happy."

"No, wait, don't."

For once, Addie listened.

"That's just what I'm afraid of."

Addie tried to understand what her mother was saying and failed. Why would anyone be afraid of being happy? "Don't you want to be happy, Mommy?"

This was where the complicated part came in, Nancy thought. "Yes, I do, very much."

Well, it seemed pretty clear-cut to Addie. "Then I'll get Guy."

It really *was* a losing battle, Nancy thought. Especially since she was fighting not only her kids and Guy, but herself, as well.

How could she make Addie understand that she was afraid to let herself be happy, to let herself enjoy being with Guy when, deep down, she knew that it could all end in the blink of an eye?

The way it had once before.

There was no way to explain it to the twins without hurting them, without exposing them to the horror that lurked out there, just beneath the joy. More than anything, she wanted to shield them from that for as long as she possibly could.

It was easier, for the time being at least, just to surrender. "Okay, go get Guy."

Addie paused only long enough to high-five A.J. before rushing off to go get the man she just *knew* was going to be her daddy as soon as Mommy stopped being so stubborn.

8

Brady Lockwood leaned a hip against the kitchen table and looked at the man he would always regard as his savior. In the background was the combined noise of his own fifteen-month-old daughter, Jamie, and the two live wires Guy had brought with him. But Brady's mind was on the woman who had accompanied the live wires.

The woman, it was very obvious to him, that his friend was in love with. Brady grinned. "So this is the one, huh?"

Brady's wife, Erin, had sent them in to get more sodas for everyone. The varieties in the refrigerator numbered as many as there were people in the house. Accustomed to making himself at home here, Guy made selections and removed the cans from their plastic rings.

He tried to sound casual in his answer. "I think so."

There was something a little guarded about the admission. Erin claimed that sensitivity to other people's feelings wasn't his strong suit, but Brady figured he was learning. "Have you told her?"

Their eyes met for a split second before Guy shrugged. "Yes."

Brady took the cans as Guy detached them and placed them on the table. "But?"

The last can freed, Guy turned around. "You know, for a physicist, you're pretty astute."

"It rubs off after being with Erin for more than a year and a half." The playful banter didn't detract from the very real gratitude he felt. "Which I wouldn't have if it wasn't for you."

Guy was never comfortable with gratitude. Though outgoing, he preferred to do and then move on. He lifted a careless shoulder now and let it drop. "Would have happened anyway."

He and Erin felt otherwise. "I don't think so." Brady loaded the cans onto a tray. There was enough here for an army. "And I'm always going to be grateful, so whatever you want, it's yours." Not that Guy would ever ask. They were alike that way, he and Guy. Asking favors wasn't in their nature. Still, Brady wanted to do something to help out what was obviously a slow-moving scenario. "Want me to put in a good word?"

Guy laughed shortly. "It's not the good words that's the problem."

Curious, Brady set down the tray again. This wasn't a conversation that could be continued with an audience. "What is, then? Last husband a bastard?'' he guessed. Guy hadn't given them any details when he called to ask if his invitation to dinner could be extended to cover a few more people.

If it had only been a matter of convincing Nancy that he was different from the man who had fathered the twins, Guy could have found a way to do it. But this was much more knotty.

"Worse. Last husband was a cop."

"Oh." Brady waited, knowing there had to be more.

"A dead cop."

"I see." Now it made sense. He understood dark fears that rose up in the night. His had haunted him when his mind, a blank slate, refused to summon up any images, even after familiar things were presented to him. He had been afraid that it would always be that way, a void empty of any memories except the most recent. "And she's afraid that it might happen again."

His own mortality was something Guy never thought about. What was written was going to be. Worrying about it wasn't going to change anything.

"Yeah, something like that."

Brady had never been an emotional man—until he lost everything and then, through the grace of God and Guy, got it back again. His credo now was to never take anything for granted.

"Hell, you shouldn't let something like that stand in your way," he said, with more feeling than Guy had heard in his voice in a long time. "Life's very precious. You should grab and hang on to whatever you can.''

His point exactly, Guy thought. "Don't tell me, tell her.''

Brady picked up the tray again and headed for the family room. "All right, I will.''

Guy grabbed his arm. "Hey, no, I was only kidding. I want her to make her mind up by herself. I think she's coming around slowly.''

The groundwork he'd been laying was beginning to come together. Guy could feel it. More than that, he could see it in Nancy's eyes. Bringing her here to see how happy his friends were was all part of the plan.

All right, Brady thought, he could respect that. In Guy's place, he'd probably say the same thing. "For what it's worth, I think she's great.''

Guy grinned like a small kid with his first two-wheeler. "Thanks. It's worth a lot.''

Erin peered into the kitchen. Nancy was right behind her. "What is taking you two so long in here?''

Erin looked at them, shaking her head. "Boy, every time Brady walks into the kitchen, he has to take a refresher course, but you,'' she said to Guy, "I'm surprised at you.'' Then, before Guy could say anything, Erin looked at Nancy. "Has he cooked for you yet?''

Nancy didn't miss the look that went between Erin and her husband. There was some kind of code here. "As a matter of fact, yes.''

"My advice then to you is to grab this man. Your taste buds will thank you for it for the rest of your life. You can share the cooking." She grinned up at Brady, love shining in her eyes. "If my husband did it, we'd share the indigestion. He burns water," she confided loudly to Nancy.

Brady shrugged, unfazed by his shortcomings. "My talents lie in other directions."

Erin grinned broadly, placing a hand on the stomach that was not yet swollen with their second child.

"Yeah, I know." There was a twinkle in her eyes that they would have needed sunglasses to miss. "I guess this is as good a time as any to make the announcement."

Because his mind was on families, Guy understood immediately. "Another one?" he cried, slapping Brady on the back.

Brady shrugged. "Hey, you get a thing right, you keep on doing it."

Guy hugged Erin, then backed off, afraid he'd gotten carried away in his enthusiasm. Pregnant women, even those who didn't look it yet, always seemed so fragile to him. "Congratulations!"

"Thank you," Erin said. Her smile softened as she looked at him. "Really."

Nancy wondered exactly what Erin meant by that as she took her turn at hugging the woman. There was obviously something that she was missing.

"Me too. Congratulations."

Addie, holding on to a wiggling Jamie, shuffled

into the kitchen. A.J. was right behind her. The grown-ups had forgotten that they were still out there, and they had come in to remind them.

"Why are you saying that to her, Mommy?" Addie asked, struggling to hold on to Erin's little girl.

Seeing her plight, Brady took his daughter into his arms.

Nancy slipped her arm around Addie. It seemed like only yesterday, Addie and A.J. were that little, and now look. "Because Erin is going to have another baby."

A.J.'s eyes shone. "So are we," he announced.

Nancy felt color drain from her face and then come flooding back, at least three shades deeper than before. "A.J.!"

Erin and Brady turned to look at Guy, but he only spread his hands out wide. If Nancy was pregnant, he'd certainly had nothing to do with it!

"Well, we are," A.J. said stubbornly. He had it on the best authority. People got married and babies came. Adam Wayne had told him that was the way it happened, and Adam should know. He was nine and a half. "As soon as you and Guy get married."

Guy laughed and hooked an arm around Nancy's waist, bringing her to him. He kissed her hair, still laughing.

"Looks to me like you've got your own cheering section right there." Brady nodded at A.J.

Guy looked at Nancy pointedly. "Yeah, but it's the principal player's decision I'm interested in."

Time to retreat, Nancy thought. She turned to Erin for help.

"Why don't I give you a hand with dinner?" She took the tray filled with cans from Erin and handed it to Guy. "Let them stay with the kids for a bit."

Erin grinned. "Hey, I could always use a hand." She waited until all five had trooped out and were well into the family room before getting down to the real business at hand: pumping Nancy for information. "I hope you know that's a very nice man you have there."

A.J. had already caused enough misunderstandings for one day. "I don't have him—"

Erin opened the oven door and slid out the pot roast. "Oh, I wouldn't take any bets on that." She reached for the pot holders and gingerly removed the roasting pan from the oven. Turning, she placed it on the counter, then spared Nancy a look. She looked scared, Erin thought. Why? "He looks pretty taken with you *and* your kids. I was beginning to think that Guy was never going to find anyone."

Studying her as she pretended to be busy with last-minute details, Erin sensed a reluctance in Nancy. There was an inner struggle going on that the woman wasn't happy about.

Erin decided to tip the scales a bit in Guy's favor. It was the least she could do, after what he had done for her. "Did he ever tell you how we all met?"

"No." Nancy hadn't thought to ask, either. Guy had just seemed enthusiastic when he asked if she and the twins would accompany him to his friends' house for dinner. Addie and A.J. had accepted for all of them before she had a chance to draw a breath. She hadn't had the heart to turn him down then. And maybe she wanted to see the sort of friends Guy had.

Erin shook her head. "Typical." Gingerly she lifted the pot roast and placed it on the platter, then moved the pan into the sink. "Guy never likes to talk about himself, or what a difference he makes in people's lives." She stopped as the magnitude of her words hit her. "He does, you know."

Yeah, he has in mine. And I'm so afraid of what that difference means. Nancy forced herself to remain casual.

But Erin suddenly sounded so serious, it aroused her curiosity. "What kind of a difference did he make in yours?"

Erin turned and wiped her hands on the kitchen towel. "He found Brady for me. Or brought him back, actually."

"Brady left you?" Brady hadn't struck her as the type to walk out on a woman, or a relationship. But then, most people wouldn't have said that she was the type to be running from one, either, and yet she was.

"Not voluntarily." Time had done little to take the edge off the pain she'd felt in those horrible months without Brady, not knowing, never really sure where he was. "We weren't married at the time, and I was pregnant and trying to find a way to tell him." A rueful smile lifted the corners of her mouth. "He wasn't keen on bringing kids into what he felt was a troubled world." It was hard to believe that was Brady. He was so different now. "You know, all the intellectual stuff you tell yourself before the fact." She began arranging tiny boiled potatoes in a ring around the pot roast. "Anyway, we had an argument before I could tell him about the baby, and he walked out."

She paused for a second, as if to brace herself against the image her words evoked.

"And disappeared from my life for five months. He was a victim of a mugging. A blow to the head gave him amnesia." She saw the mute, horrified look on Nancy's face. "Guy found him wandering around the next day, no wallet, no ID."

But why had they been separated for five months? It didn't make sense. "You reported him missing, didn't you?"

Erin had berated herself a hundred times in those months for not doing just that.

"Not at first. He was supposed to leave on a business trip the next day," she explained quickly. "I just thought he was still angry and left without saying goodbye. When he didn't return, I thought something had happened to him at his destination. I was frantic and flew up to San Francisco to try to find him." She smiled ruefully at the futile effort. "He was here all the time."

And if it weren't for Guy, they could have gone on living here, in the same city, and never meeting. She didn't even want to think about that.

Erin cleared her throat, dissolving the lump that was there. "Anyway, the reason I'm telling you all this is because Guy didn't just take Brady to the police station and then to the hospital, he took him to Demi."

"Demi? His sister?"

Erin nodded. "She gave Brady a job, and a place to stay behind the restaurant. Guy could have stopped right there. He didn't even have to do that much. But instead, he never gave up trying to find out who Brady was." She took the salad she'd made earlier out of the refrigerator and placed it on the table beside the pot roast platter. "It was Guy's grandmother who read the personal ad I placed in the paper." The ad had been a shot in the dark, her last attempt at locating Brady. It had just been a simple plea:

Brady, Come home, Love, Erin.

"But if he didn't know his name, how did Guy know that the ad was for Brady?"

"Brady had a medallion I gave him. It was inscribed with our names. Thank God," she added as an afterthought. It was funny how things just seemed to hook up sometimes. And how they didn't, at other times. She felt it was her duty to prod Nancy a little. Guy had brought the woman here for a reason.

"You see, up to that time, I thought that maybe Brady just dropped out of sight on purpose. Guy brought us together, and then stuck around to help." She smiled fondly as she spoke of the man. "Guy never lost touch with Brady, or me. He was best man at our wedding, and our baby's godfather. So you can see why I'm so crazy about him."

Nancy nodded. "I get the picture." She tried to imagine herself in Erin's place, and shuddered. To look at the petite woman, no one would have dreamed that she'd ever been through her own personal hell. Nancy supposed that gave them something in common. "But Brady remembers everything now, doesn't he?"

"Yes, fortunately. But in my heart I know he wouldn't, if it hadn't been for Guy's intervention." Erin topped off the gravy bowl. "Not everyone puts themselves out like that."

"I know." No doubt about it, the man in the next room was exceptional.

Brady poked his head in. "Hey, about the pot calling the kettle black—" His mouth twitched. He knew exactly what his wife was up to.

"We're coming, we're coming," Erin called out. "Keep your pants on."

Her command was met with giggles from A.J. The laughter was infectious. Erin heard her daughter chiming in.

"That's some charmer you have there," she told Nancy.

"I'll take that as a compliment," Guy said, coming up behind her. Timing it just right, he relieved her of the platter. As he turned to walk into the dining room with his prize, he winked at Nancy.

And set her pulse racing.

It was incredible, she thought as she followed the procession, bringing in the gravy. She had the same reaction to his wink every time. She wondered if it would always be that way.

"I liked your friends," Nancy confided as she got out of the car. Opening the rear door behind her, she reached in to take Addie into her arms. It was late, and both children had fallen asleep on the ride home.

She wouldn't be able to do this much longer, she thought. Addie and A.J. would soon be too heavy to carry.

A baby might be nice, she mused. Like Jamie. A baby with curly black hair.

She stopped herself before her thoughts got carried away.

"I'm glad, because they certainly liked you." Guy gently lifted A.J. The boy stirred and tucked his arm around Guy's neck. The swell he felt within his chest had already been identified and labeled. It was love. He was in love with all of them, and it was a terrific feeling.

Guy followed Nancy to her door. "You know, my parents are going to have a big party, celebrating their thirtieth anniversary next month. They'd love to meet you."

Plans. He was making plans. Long-range plans. And they involved her. It both thrilled her and scared the hell out of her.

The full import of his words sank in as she shifted Addie to one side and fished out her key. "They know about me?"

Guy took the key from her and opened the door. She was having too much trouble juggling child and key. "Demi talked."

Had he said something to Demi about them? "But we only met once. How would she—?"

Guy flipped on the light and went directly to the twins' bedroom. "Demi wants to see me married— it would take the pressure off her for a while."

Though true, that was only partially the reason Demi had said anything to their mother and grandmother. Demi was as sure about Nancy as he was. The only one who wasn't sure about Nancy was Nancy.

Nancy waited until he set A.J. on the bed, and then passed Addie to him. It was impossible for her to reach up to the top bunk with the little girl. But Guy could manage easily.

She smiled. "I never thought of myself as a relief for pressure before."

"I do." Turning, he grazed the side of her temple

with the softest of kisses. Its impact was all the greater for it. "A great relief. Soon."

The promise whispered along her skin.

"About soon..." Nancy began fifteen minutes later.

"Yes?" As he asked, he caught her wrist and turned her around so that she was forced to press her back against the wall. Leaning in, Guy placed a hand on the wall on either side of her, framing her.

She did love him, she thought. There was no use denying it. But there were other options open to people in love, options other than marriage. Safer options, as far as the heart was concerned.

Nancy tried to collect her thoughts, and her courage. "Couldn't we just become lovers?"

Her stomach was doing horrendous flip-flops as she asked the question. All the while, as they put Addie and A.J. to bed, she had tried not to dwell on how perfect that felt, to be there with him and them. Just like a family. Because they weren't. And they wouldn't be. But if, for a while, they enjoyed one another, what was the harm in that?

She felt herself growing limp as Guy feathered kisses along her forehead. Nancy dug her fingers into his arms to steady herself.

"Just?" Guy echoed, pressing a kiss to her throat. "There's no such thing as just lovers." Raising his head, he looked at Nancy. "You mean instead of getting married?"

She nodded, though exactly how she managed to move anything when all her limbs were weak she wasn't entirely sure.

Still not there, he thought. But he was getting closer.

He toyed with her earring, watching in fascination as Nancy's pupils grew large. Unable to resist, he kissed her again before answering.

"Not that that's not the greatest offer I've ever had, Nancy, but I'm a greedy sort of guy. I want it all." As if punctuating his statement, he kissed her again, long and hard and with just a hint of the passion that had taken over his soul. His passion for her. "I want to marry you, Nancy," he whispered against her mouth.

"Guy, I'm afraid."

"Not of me, Nancy."

She could taste his tongue as it moved along her lips, teasing her.

"Never of me."

The room had turned pitch-black and was spinning. She knew it was useless to hope that it was merely an earthquake. "I can't think when you're doing that."

She felt his grin against her mouth before he kissed her again.

"That's the idea. Don't think, Nancy, don't ponder this out." Progressively warmer kisses fanned out along the planes of her face, her throat, the outline of her ear. "It's not an exercise in philosophy.

This is about you and me, and the kids. Our kids. All of them.''

Somehow, Nancy moved her head back. Sucking air into her lungs, she braced herself against his arms. The room settled down a little, but not much.

What was he saying?

"All of them?" she repeated, bewildered. At last count, she'd had two.

He grinned, holding her to him. Feeling the wild beating of her heart and taking comfort in it. "Well, I plan to add to the number. Not right away, of course. Two's a good start. But eventually..."

Maybe she was crazy, saying no. Self preservation was slipping down a myriad of notches at a drastic pace. "You're making this very hard to resist."

It was what he wanted to hear. "Good, then don't. We can have the reception at the restaurant."

Her eyes widened. "Whoa," she warned. "I haven't said yes yet."

He knew better. "Yes, you have. Your eyes have." A fragment of a melody played in his head, transcending the years. "There's yes in your eyes, Nancy." Lightly, he outlined the shape of a heart on her breast, making the tingle that rose within her almost unbearable. "And in your heart. Your mind will just have to come around."

She knew there were reasons, good reasons, why she was resisting. Why she *should* be resisting. But for the life of her, she couldn't think of a single one.

Her mind was all smoky, cloudy, and he was the cause of that.

She swallowed, knowing she was asking for trouble. Knowing she couldn't help herself. "Maybe you'd like to convince me some more?"

"Hey, best offer I've had all day." His lips hovered just a breath from hers. He could feel her against him, could feel her yearning. It matched his own. "Maybe all my life," he whispered just before he kissed her.

She had no one to blame for this but herself, Nancy thought, staring at a screen that had nothing but her byline on it. She'd let it happen, walking right into it with her eyes wide open. Well, partially open. And there were penalties to pay, just waiting for her.

She knew all that, but she still couldn't help grinning like an idiot.

Love did that to a person, she mused.

She didn't feel like writing. She felt like sitting and doodling. Writing Guy's name over and over again, then encircling it with a heart.

Nancy tried to be stern with herself. She couldn't behave like some lovesick teenager, she had responsibilities. And a column to do.

A column that she hadn't a single idea for, she thought ruefully. And why? Because her head was crowded with thoughts of Guy. Crowded with snippets of moments that they'd shared together.

Ever since she walked into her kitchen and saw him standing there, looking better than any man had a right to in a pair of ordinary bathing trunks, she'd been heading toward this. Toward the inevitable.

Toward marrying him.

She might as well resign herself to that.

Nancy grinned. Now if she could just manage to turn that into a column somehow, everything would be perfect.

"Mommy, come quick."

She closed her eyes and sighed. "A.J., I'm working. You know the rules."

They weren't supposed to bother her, although they usually did, at least twice a column. But today was different. She was really in danger of missing her deadline if she didn't do some serious writing here.

"But, Mommy, this is important."

Nancy pushed away from her desk. They weren't going to stop until she came out there and saw what they were up to.

"One of you had better be bleeding," she muttered under her breath.

"Quick, Mommy." Addie added her voice to her brother's. Both were unusually urgent.

Maybe something was wrong, she thought, hurrying out. But when she walked into the living room, the twins were standing in front of the television set. She felt her temper rising.

"All right, what's the big emergency?" she demanded.

"Look!" Addie and A.J. both pointed toward the set. "Guy's on TV!"

9

"Guy?" Nancy asked dumbly, unable, unwilling to process the information. "Are you sure?"

"Yes!" Addie was jumping up and down as she pointed to the TV screen. "They just showed Guy's picture. They said he was there, talking to some bad man. This is on everywhere, Mommy."

To prove it, Addie began flipping channels. A different shot of the same scene kept flashing across the screen as she went from one channel to another in rapid succession.

In a trance, Nancy drew closer. She took the remote control away from Addie, barely looking at her daughter. She couldn't take her eyes off the screen.

"Is Guy famous?" A.J. wanted to know. "Like Big Bird?"

Addie poked A.J. in the ribs. "No, he's more famous. He's a people. People are always more famous than birds and animals." With a shake of her head, she turned to Nancy. "Right, Mommy?"

But Nancy didn't answer. Unable to look away, she waved her hand at the twins to tell them to be quiet. It was hard enough to hear anything over the thundering of her heart as it pounded in her chest, without having Addie and A.J. compete for her attention.

A tingling numbness descended over her body. How could this be happening?

The usual afternoon sitcom reruns that the twins were fond of watching over and over again had been preempted by a late-breaking news bulletin.

There was a knot forming in her stomach as she listened. It was pulling so hard and so tight, Nancy could barely breathe.

It took every bit of concentration for her to hear anything. A strange buzzing in her ears was blocking out what the newscaster was saying. Her hand shaking, Nancy pressed the volume control on the remote.

The twins, sensing that what was unfolding on the screen was different from the serious programs Mommy let them watch sometimes, fell into silence. Instinctively drawing toward one another for comfort, they mutely watched the screen.

A tall, handsome newscaster was reporting live from the scene, dramatizing every word he delivered. It was obvious that he was repeating a report he had previously given and was attempting to find a new slant to it.

A new slant to the report that concerned the fate of the man she loved.

"Once again, viewers, we're reporting live from

Huntington Beach, just outside of The Margarita, a popular restaurant with the local citizens, where a real-life drama is going on. It was just a little more than an hour ago when a high-speed chase that began in East L.A. ended right here when the suspect, presumably out of gas, suddenly careened off the freeway and pulled up in front of the restaurant.''

Pausing for effect, the newscaster turned and allowed the technician handling the camcorder to pan the area right behind him. Nancy saw the sawhorses that had been hastily thrown up by the police department. Behind them, or hanging off them, people were waving and mugging for the camera.

Mugging while Guy was risking his life. Nancy pressed her lips together to keep from crying out and frightening the twins.

Slowly, the newscaster turned back to the camera. "He ran in here just before the two officers pursuing him could catch up. Right now, the owner and presumably several of the employees are being held hostage behind those closed doors. Ironically, the restaurant was just closing for its midday break when the gunman entered.''

Another pregnant pause followed before the man continued. "Police have surrounded the area, cordoning it off. Presently, one brave man in blue is negotiating with the suspect. I'm told he's trying to secure the release of the hostages by offering himself in exchange.'' Solemn eyes turned to look straight into the camera. "Everyone is praying that Officer Tripopulous succeeds in his noble efforts."

No!

Snapping to life, Nancy's mind screamed the word over and over again. No, it couldn't be happening, not again. She couldn't stand it if it happened again.

Afraid she had said the word aloud, or that the sobs she felt building in her chest would break free, Nancy covered her mouth with her hands. She didn't want to frighten Addie and A.J.

Most of all, she didn't want to be frightened herself. But she was. She was oh, so frightened.

She had to get there.

Her head pounding, her thoughts scattered in all directions, Nancy tried to think. Who was home? She couldn't take the children with her, she had to find someone to leave them with. But who did she know who was available at this hour?

Erin.

Her hands were visibly shaking as she punched Erin's telephone number into the keypad. Twice she hit the wrong numbers and had to start over again. Out of the corner of her eye, Nancy saw the twins silently watching her.

For their sake, she tried to smile. "It's okay, kids. It's okay."

No, it wasn't. It wasn't okay. Guy was out there, risking his life, maybe living the last few minutes of it, while she was fumbling with a telephone number.

The telephone on the other end of the line began to ring. Nancy twisted the cord around her fingers. *Please be home. Please be home.*

Erin answered on the fourth ring, and barely had time to say hello before Nancy began talking. "Erin, I'm so glad you're home. This is Nancy. Guy's—"

Nancy didn't need to explain. She heard an ocean of sympathy in the other woman's voice. "Oh, Nancy, I just turned on the TV—"

Nancy didn't let her finish. There was no time for sympathy. There might be no time left at all.

Turning away from the twins, she lowered her voice. "I'm going crazy just watching. I've got to be there. Erin, can I leave the kids with you?"

There wasn't even a moment's hesitation. "Of course. Bring them right over."

"I'll be there as soon as I can." Hanging up, Nancy paused only long enough to grab her purse.

"Why are we going to see Erin again, Mommy?" Addie wanted to know. There was a nervous tremor in her voice, as if she were trying very hard to understand what was happening.

"I need to be somewhere right now, Addie." Nancy hustled them both into the car. "And Erin is going to mind you while I'm gone."

"Are you going to go and help Guy?" A.J. asked.

She willed herself to be calm. She couldn't drive like a maniac with her kids in the car. Couldn't go racing up to the scene the way she wanted to.

"I only wish I could, honey."

"Is he going to be all right, Mommy?" Addie asked in a small voice.

With one hand on the wheel, Nancy stroked Addie's head. She tried to give her daughter the assurance that she couldn't give herself. "He's going to be fine, Addie."

Please, God, don't let me be lying to my kids.

She was oddly hollow-eyed as she drove from Erin's house up to Huntington Beach. If she didn't think, didn't feel, she could get through this.

The traffic whizzed by her, just as it would have any other day. Just as if something horrible weren't happening a matter of a few miles away.

Hands tight on the wheel, eyes straight ahead, Nancy hardly saw any of the cars around her. She'd switched from the station she usually listened to one that only broadcasted the news.

It was all she could do to manage to keep the mounting hysteria she felt from breaking through. She found herself having to ease off the gas pedal every few minutes. The sense of urgency running through her flowed to her feet, making her press the accelerator to the floor. Cars moved out of her way as she changed from one lane to another and then back again.

Oh, God, what if she was too late? The thought choked her.

Nancy knew exactly where the restaurant was located. It was almost at the foot of the freeway off-ramp. She'd even stopped there once or twice herself. Vaguely she recalled that the restaurant had been the scene of a robbery a couple of years ago. Two men had driven off the freeway, robbed the owner and gotten away, all within fifteen minutes. They'd never been caught.

You'd think the owner would have closed down after that.

Why hadn't he closed down? she demanded tearfully. He was just asking for trouble.

She blinked back the tears that obscured her vision.

Oh, God, she had to find a way to get Guy away from there, before anything happened to him. She felt sorry for the people inside the restaurant, but she didn't know them.

She knew Guy. And if anything happened to him... Nancy couldn't bring herself to finish the sentence, not even in her own mind.

Suddenly, Nancy's heart froze. The soft-spoken newscaster was informing his audience that it appeared that the ''negotiating officer has succeeded in getting the gunman to let him in. Ladies and gentlemen,'' he said, excitement pulsating in his voice, ''the hostages are being sent out. He did it!''

''Now get yourself out, damn it!'' Nancy shouted at the radio.

This was exactly what she'd been afraid of, exactly what she had warned herself against. And here she was, going through hell all over again.

Please keep him safe, she prayed. *Please.*

Tears were streaming down her face by the time she drove off the freeway. The scene of the siege was a madhouse. There were squad cars and news vans parked everywhere, choking off the area.

Nancy abandoned her car in the first available space she could find. Her lungs, already aching, felt as if they were going to burst as she ran to the perimeter of the police barricade. Elbowing her way through, she managed to get up to the front of the sawhorse closest to the restaurant. From where she was, the restaurant was less than sixty feet away.

But as she tried to crawl under the sawhorse, a pair of strong arms stopped her.

An older, heavyset patrolman shook his head and moved her back behind the barricade.

"Sorry, lady, nobody crosses the line." Exasperation deepened the lines on his forehead. "Can't you see there's a hostage situation going on?"

No, her mind cried, all she saw was Guy. All she saw was that he might get killed, just as Tom had.

As the policeman turned away, she grabbed him by his shirtsleeve. "Please, I have to see Guy."

The policeman's face softened. Sympathy entered his eyes as he realized that the woman before him was not just another crime-scene groupie, but someone who knew one of them. It humanized her.

"I'm afraid he's not available right now," he told her gently.

"I know he's not available right now," she cried.

"But you've got to get him out of there." She was begging now. "Get him out of there before he gets...hurt." She choked on the word.

The hand that was on her shoulder was no longer a restraining one. Rather, there was comfort in the pressure she felt from his fingers.

"He'll be okay, ma'am."

He said it as if he believed it, Nancy thought. They were all crazy, every last one of them. Crazy.

"He knows what he's doing. Guy's got a charmed life."

Tom had thought that, too, until the charm ran out.

The officer began moving away from her. "Best thing you can do for Guy right now is pray."

Nancy looked up at the policeman, tears shining in her eyes. "What do you think I have been doing?" she asked hoarsely.

He merely nodded as he left.

The policeman was wrong, she thought, staring at the front of the restaurant. The best thing she could do for both of them was to walk away.

But she couldn't. All she could do was stand here, like the others, and watch. And, unlike the others, die a little inside.

She became aware of everything, the sun baking on her shoulders, the dissonance of the crowd, the still life that the front of the restaurant had become. Time crawled by on aching, arthritic legs as first five minutes, then ten, then fifteen, went by.

Wasn't he ever coming out?

When she heard the gunshot, Nancy shrieked. Guy had left his gun behind when he went in. The man on the radio had made a big deal of it, as if it had been done for the sole purpose of adding color to his report. The only one armed within that restaurant was the other man.

Had he killed Guy?

Half-crazy with fear, Nancy ducked under the barricade and dashed out, running toward the restaurant.

The door opened just as the policeman who'd talked to her earlier caught up with Nancy. They both froze, their eyes fixed on the door. Everyone was watching to see what would happen next.

It was like a dream, a surrealistic dream. Holding her breath, Nancy saw Guy emerge from the darkened restaurant. Beside him was the suspect, handcuffed and subdued. The man, long-haired and scraggly, taller than Guy, was hanging his head.

Policemen converged around the pair, taking Guy's prisoner. Someone clapped Guy on the back.

He saw her immediately.

Somehow, throughout the ordeal, he'd had a feeling that Nancy was out here, waiting for him. When he walked outside with his prisoner, he'd been searching the crowd for her.

Nancy was in his arms in a heartbeat, sobbing his name, touching him to make sure he was whole. "Did he hurt you?"

"No."

Exhaustion and triumph was etched on his face, beneath the sweat. He cupped the back of her head, kissing her mouth hard. She'd never tasted sweeter than she did at this very moment. Life had never tasted sweeter.

Holding her, he breathed in her fragrance. Guy was only partially aware of the officers who passed before him with the prisoner. "Go easy on him," he called to them. "He gave himself up."

Nancy didn't understand. "But the gunshot. I heard him fire his gun."

Guy shook his head. "He dropped it as he was handing it to me." Because it was over, because no one was hurt, he was able to smile about it now. Holding her against him, he blew out a long breath. "So, how was your day?"

"Lousy." Nancy was shaking, shaking so hard she could barely stand. Guy understood. He held her for a long moment, cradling her against his body. He brushed a kiss over her hair.

"Yeah, I know. I know."

Somehow, she managed to wedge her hands between them. With her last scrap of strength, she pushed him back away from her. He stared at her in bewildered surprise.

"No, you don't," she said hoarsely. "You don't know. You don't have a clue."

She swallowed, afraid she would cry again. But

when Guy tried to take her back in his arms she wouldn't allow it.

"I just went through hell. Do you know what it felt like, to have the kids call me into the room and see that you were plastered all over the channels like the disaster flavor of the month?"

"Made all the channels, huh?" Guy asked glibly, trying to downplay the incident until she calmed down.

Anger flared, red-hot and painful. "It's not funny, Guy."

"No," he agreed evenly. "It's not." What did she want from him? He did what he was paid to do. Save lives. They stared at one another, at an impasse. "Hey, I was scared, too. But I just couldn't leave them in there." Fighting a fear that had no name, he tried desperately to make her understand. "Nancy, those people in there, they could have been Demi and Brady. Or my parents. Or my grandparents. I had to try something. That kid was desperate and wild-eyed when he ran in there." He saw the question enter her eyes. "I was at the cross street when he flew by in his car. I've seen that look before." And every time he did, it sent chills down his spine. Desperate men did desperate things. "There was no telling what he might have been capable of."

"Like killing you." She hit his shoulder then, with the flat of her hand, hard. Her palm stung. "He could have killed you," she repeated. Frustrated, her eyes boring into him, she hit him again.

Guy caught her wrist the third time. "Enough, Nancy," he said sternly.

Hot tears bubbled and overflowed. "Yes, enough. I've had enough. I can't do this."

His nerves raw, Guy didn't understand what she was talking about. "Do what?"

Suddenly, there were microphones being shoved in his face.

"Officer, over here!" someone called. "Can we have a word for our viewers?" More microphones were joined by more disembodied voices, swarming around them until they were completely surrounded.

"Not now," Guy growled.

Holding tightly on to Nancy, Guy elbowed his way through the wall of reporters and camera people closing in on them. Policemen came to part the crowd, giving them safe passage by acting as a human shield.

As soon as he had her off to the side, Guy looked at Nancy. He held on to her arm, afraid that if he let go, he'd lose her.

"Do what?" he repeated, as if there had been no interruption. His eyes had grown steely. His nerves were drawn out so tightly they were on the verge of snapping.

As were hers, he thought, looking into her eyes. Taking a deep breath, he let go of her.

"I can't go on seeing you," she answered. The

words were barely above a whisper. Her throat was dry. As dry as her eyes were wet.

He couldn't believe he'd heard her correctly. But he must have. She was crying and backing away from him. "Nancy, don't do this."

She closed her eyes, trying to seal in the pain. It wouldn't leave. She'd been so afraid, so very afraid. She was still afraid.

Nancy looked at him. "I could say the same thing to you."

He placed his hands on her shoulders. They were talking about his turning his back on his identity. "Nancy, I'm a policeman. It's what I do."

She pulled away. "And I worry. It's what I do." He knew the danger he lived with on a daily basis. Couldn't he see what it would be like for her, being married to him? To his badge? "I don't want to die a little every time you go out the door, Guy, worrying that you might not come back."

He only knew one way around that. "Then don't worry."

She shook her head. He was asking the impossible. "It's not that easy."

"Yes," he insisted, "it is." He had to make her see reason. "Nancy, worrying never changed anything. Things either happen, or they don't. Worrying about them is just a waste of energy. Energy that could be put to better use."

He wasn't getting through to her. Desperate, his voice picked up speed. "Look, I can't promise you that I'll live forever. No one can do that. But we have something special. And a little bit of something wonderful is better than a lifetime of nothing at all.''

She wasn't saying anything. He was losing her. Guy played the last card he had. "Do you regret marrying your husband?"

Tom had been her childhood sweetheart. He'd given her two beautiful babies. How could Guy even suggest that she regretted marrying him?

"Of course not."

He looked into her eyes, making her a promise. "And you won't regret marrying me."

But she turned her head when he tried to kiss her. If he kissed her, she'd weaken. And she couldn't. She needed all her strength to do this.

"I can't turn it off like that. I just can't. If I love you, it comes in the package."

"If?" he echoed. How could she even question what they had? "Nancy, you do love me."

She lifted her head, fighting back tears again. "I can get over it."

His eyes narrowed. What he'd just been through was nothing compared to what the thought of Nancy leaving him was doing to him.

"Just like that?"

Nancy shook her head. "No," she answered slowly, "not just like that. But with effort, and in time."

Guy struggled to hold on to his temper. "More wasted effort. Nancy, we have something precious here. I want to hang on to it. It doesn't happen for everyone, but it happened for us. You can't just throw that away.''

She had to get away from him before she broke down completely. She knew what she was doing was right. But it didn't make it any easier to do.

"I'm sorry. I really am. But I've got the kids to think of. They were too young to remember losing Tom.'' She searched his face for some shred of understanding. "But they're older now. They won't be too young to remember losing you. I can't do that to them. Or me.''

He refused to believe her. Nancy couldn't walk out on him. She wouldn't, not when they loved each other. "How about to us? Can you do that to us?''

Her lips were trembling as she pressed them together. "I'm sorry, Guy,'' she whispered again. *More than you'll ever know.* "I really am.''

Very slowly, she turned and began to walk away on someone else's legs. Legs that felt like leaden tree trunks.

"I'm not giving up,'' he called after her. "Do you hear me, Nancy? I'm not giving up.''

She didn't answer him.

She couldn't.

With effort, she just kept walking, and prayed that he wouldn't follow her.

He didn't.

Her heart broke long before she reached her car.

10

He made it easy for her.

And damn hard, at the same time.

She didn't have to try to avoid Guy. As far as she could tell, he wasn't there. Or, if he was, he was keeping to himself. There was no music coming from his apartment, no sound of his car pulling up into the carport, signaling his return from work.

No softly whistled tune as he came up the walk past her window on his way to his apartment.

Her life was absolutely Guy-free, just as she had wanted.

And she was absolutely miserable.

Nancy tried her best to come to terms with the turn her life had taken, to concentrate on what was really important to her. But after six days of this, what was really important to her was suffering. Her kids were noticeably unhappy, and her columns just didn't seem to have the zip, the wit, she had come to be known for.

Writing even a few words had gone from being ridiculously easy to just pure agony. Instead of an hour or so, she felt as if she were glued in front of her computer all day.

With nothing to show for it.

Maybe she needed something to eat, Nancy thought in exasperation after the latest two-hour session had yielded exactly one sentence. These days, she'd lost her appetite, and she had to rely on the clock, rather than hunger pains, to let her know when she should be feeding the twins. If it weren't for them, she'd forget to eat herself. Nothing seemed to taste right anymore.

"So how's it going?" Nancy asked briskly as she walked out into the kitchen.

Amid scattered papers and books, Addie and A.J. were planted at the table, frowning identical frowns at their homework assignments.

Addie merely shrugged, for once uninterested in trying to top her brother and crow that she was almost done with her work, while he was still plodding through the first math problem.

"Not as good as when Guy was helping us," A.J. told his mother. He looked up at her, sheer misery in his eyes. "Doesn't he like us anymore?"

"I'm sure he does, honey." Nancy debated taking the banana back with her, then abandoned it in the fruit bowl. It probably wasn't ripe enough yet, anyway.

A.J. cocked his head. What Mommy had said still didn't seem right to him. "If he likes us, then why doesn't he come over anymore?"

How many times did she have to say the same thing to them before they understood?

Nancy struggled to rein in her temper. It wasn't their fault. It was nobody's fault.

Except maybe hers.

Turning around, she leaned back against the counter and looked at the twins. "Because Guy and I have decided not to see each other anymore."

Actually, I decided, and he hasn't done anything about it, she thought dejectedly.

Addie leaned her chin on her fisted hand, her eyes just shy of being accusing. She had really liked Guy. "You don't love him?"

Nancy had never lied to them, and she didn't intend to start now. "Yes, I love him."

The expression on her daughter's face told Nancy that Addie thought this was getting really weird. "Doesn't he love you?"

Nancy thought of the way Guy had held her, close, so that their heartbeats melded into one. Of the way he had kissed her, slow and tender, shaking her right down to her very essence.

"Yes, he does," Nancy whispered.

Addie and A.J. exchanged confused looks. "Then why, Mommy?" A.J. asked. "Why aren't you and Guy together anymore?"

He sounded so grown-up when he asked, Nancy thought with a pang. All too soon, her son and her daughter were going to be involved in this very same rigmarole of hearts and hurts.

And what kind of a life partner would she wish for her children? Someone who was kind and loving, someone who knew when to laugh and when to sympathize.

Someone, she thought, swallowing the lump in her throat, who was a lot like Guy. A man she was rejecting out of fear.

Straightening, Nancy waved a hand in dismissal at the question. Maybe it was time to get back to work.

As if she could work, she thought ruefully.

"It's very complicated."

Addie knew what that meant. "Grown-up talk for she's not going to tell us," she told A.J., who looked very put out by the evasion.

Nancy stopped in the doorway of her room. The column could wait a few minutes. God knew it wasn't going anywhere, anyway. Crossing back to the kitchen, she sat down between them and looked from one to the other. They were almost a perfect hybrid of Tom and her. Sometimes, she ached just to look at them.

"Do you two remember your daddy?"

Addie looked contrite as she shook her head. The man whose framed photograph was in their room had long since ceased evoking any real memories for her, just a few hazy half dreams she didn't really remember once she was awake.

A.J. hesitated, chewing on his lip. There was a memory, a very dim one he liked to think about when he was afraid late at night and Addie was asleep. It made him feel better. Braver.

"A little," he told her.

Pleasure filled her. Nancy reached for his hand, covering it. "Oh? What do you remember?"

"He had a big lap. And a big hug." It made A.J. smile just to say it. "Like Guy."

Nancy sighed and nodded. If the similarity ended there, it would have been all right. But it didn't. "And, like Guy, he was a policeman."

Addie shifted impatiently in her chair. "We know that."

Choosing the right words to make them understand wasn't easy, but she had to try. "And you also remember that Daddy died saving people, right?"

"Right!" A.J. declared. Some of his enthusiasm left his face when Addie said nothing. He became a little fidgety, stealing a look at his mother. "But that was a good thing, right?"

She wanted to make them proud, not resentful, but Nancy also wanted them to understand her feelings. They had a right to that. And she had a right to their support.

"Yes," she agreed, "a good thing for the people he saved. But not such a good thing for us. For us, it was a bad thing. When he…" Nancy searched for a euphemism, a word that wouldn't hurt. "When he went away, I was very, very sad. If that happens to Guy, I'm going to be very sad again. I don't want to be sad again." She looked from one small, serious face to the other, hoping for a spark of understanding. "Do you see what I'm trying to say, kids?"

With the heart of a woman, Addie nodded. "It's okay, Mommy. Maybe someone else will come. Someone else you can love," she said, with the encouragement reserved for the very young and hopeful.

But A.J. was still confused, still unconvinced and still very loyal to Guy. He looked at his mother thoughtfully. "Aren't you sad now, Mommy?"

Nancy could only laugh softly. A.J. was more sensitive to her feelings than Addie was. "Yes, I guess I am."

He shook his head, more confused than ever. "Doesn't seem to be a difference," he muttered to himself.

Maybe not, she thought, getting up.

Nancy walked back into her room and sat down in front of the computer. Instead of writing, she leaned back in the swivel chair and rocked, thinking.

Out of the mouths of babes.

The phrase was no sooner in her mind than she remembered that Guy had used the same expression what seemed like a hundred years ago. When he was trying to convince her that they belonged together.

Maybe they did.

Too late.

* * *

It was time, the twins decided after a hasty conference, to take things into their own hands again. Retreating into their room where they could go about their plan unobserved, they wrote a note to Guy.

Once finished, Addie acted as lookout, promising to keep Mommy busy if she came out of her room, while A.J. slipped the note under Guy's door. They reasoned that he had to come home sometime.

A.J. wanted to knock and talk to him, but Addie didn't think that was a good idea.

Besides, she pointed out sadly, "Maybe he's really gone forever."

A.J. hated it when Addie thought bad things. It always made him feel nervous. But this time, he was sure she was wrong. She had to be.

"No, he wouldn't go away forever. He'd say goodbye first," A.J. insisted with the faith of a true believer. "Guy's just being like Mommy. Sad. When people are sad, they stay away."

Addie was unconvinced. She gave him a cold stare. "How would you know?"

"TV," he answered glibly.

Made sense to her. TV was smarter than they were. "Oh. Okay."

Then, like two small hunters, the twins waited for their prey to come out of the brush and take their bait.

* * *

"Mommy, Mommy, look, someone left this ransom note." Addie enunciated the word carefully in the midst of her breathless delivery.

She and A.J. had been wrestling on the floor next to the door over who got to work the remote control this time. Giving themselves up to the fray, they had completely displaced the scatter rug thrown there. That was when they had found the treasured piece of paper from Guy. All warfare had ceased, and now they were galvanized into a team again.

With the air of a messenger on an urgent mission, Addie thrust the note at Nancy.

A.J. was shifting from foot to foot, so excited that he hadn't even protested when Addie snatched the note out of his hand and ran into Mommy's room. He'd been the one to find it first.

Nancy turned from her desk. She had been fighting with a column all day and had only this moment put the final period in. The world wasn't a very amusing place for her these days.

But she had made her decision and, for better or worse, there was no turning back.

Guy had obviously accepted the situation. He hadn't come to her, the way he'd promised as she walked away from him at the hostage site, and tried to make her change her mind. There could be only one reason for it. He had decided she wasn't worth the trouble.

And who could blame him? It was hard on a man to be rejected so completely.

No, this was all for the best, Nancy told herself adamantly.

Now if she could only convince that hard lump of clay that lay so heavily in her chest, beating only sporadically, everything would be all right.

She took a deep breath, pushed the print sequence on her computer keyboard and gave the twins her full attention. Something she had been withholding this past week, she thought ruefully. She saw the piece of paper Addie was waving.

"Another game, Addie?" She tried to smile. It was an effort that didn't quite succeed. "Mommy really doesn't feel like playing right now."

But Addie shook her head, unwilling to be dismissed or ignored. "No, it's not a game," she insisted with feeling. "We found it under the rug when we were wrestling just now."

Nancy raised a brow. Sometimes she felt as if she were just talking to herself. "What did I tell you about wrestling?"

"You said not to," Addie parroted, as if she were repeating a jingle for breakfast cereal. What Mommy had said about wrestling wasn't important right now, this was. "Mommy, read this. I think it must be *really* important," she said breathlessly.

An actress for sure, Nancy thought fondly. Addie had all the makings of one. With a smile, she reached for the paper. "All right, let me see it."

As she opened the folded paper to read it, Addie

and A.J. clustered around her, looking over her shoulder as if they hadn't already read it themselves.

"Read it out loud," A.J. instructed.

Still thinking that it was a game, Nancy looked dutifully down at the note. She was surprised to see that instead of the wide scrawl that her children so proudly referred to as writing, she was looking at the bold letters of a masculine hand.

"Read it out loud," Addie entreated again, when her mother stared at the note in silence.

Nancy cleared her throat. It felt oddly dry. "'If you ever want to see Guy Tripopulous alive again, come to the northernmost bench in Cedarwood Park at exactly five o'clock this afternoon. Bring two small blond children in unmarked T-shirts with you. If you do not come at the appointed time, you will never see Guy again.'"

The northernmost bench in Cedarwood Park. Cedarwood Park—how it all had begun for them.

Very slowly, Nancy folded the note. He meant it, she thought. If she didn't come, she'd never see him again. He would disappear from her life.

Permanently.

In an instant, she made her decision. She didn't want to be without him permanently. She wanted, God help her, whatever she could get. If it was just a day, then it would be just a day. But whatever it was, she wanted it with Guy.

Nancy looked at her watch. It was four-thirty. Cedarwood Park was fifteen minutes away by car. Normally, they could make it easily. But at this time of day, the streets of Bedford tended to get crowded with people returning home from work. They might be cutting it close.

She rose to her feet quickly. "C'mon, we've got to get going."

Happiness filled the small bedroom.

"Then you'll see him?" A.J. cried. He'd known it all the time, but it was nice to be proven right. Especially with Addie looking on.

"Of course we'll see him." Five o'clock. What if they didn't make it on time? She looked at Addie. "Why didn't you show this to me earlier?"

"We only found it just now, Mommy," A.J. explained for his sister. "It must have gotten stuck under the rug when he pushed it under the door." A.J. began to worry his lower lip.

Addie gave A.J. a grateful look. Sometimes he could be nice. For a brother.

"Honest, Mommy," she added.

If she'd straightened up the way she meant to, she might have found the note earlier, Nancy thought. She might already be on her way.

There was no time to debate the failings of her housekeeping. She had a man to get to. Grabbing her purse and her children, she headed for the door.

"Mommy, you forgot to turn off your computer." A.J. pointed behind him as they left the apartment.

"Later." She rushed them to the car. She couldn't

worry about minor things like electric bills at a time like this.

He'd taken an hour of personal time and had left the precinct early.

So that he could sit on this bench and stew, Guy thought darkly. So that he could sit here and listen to the sound of his heart being broken, bit by bit.

Served him right for being a fool.

He nodded absently as a woman smiled at him, hurrying by with her daughter. He didn't see her. He saw Nancy and Addie. Everywhere he looked, he saw Nancy, only to discover it was just his mind playing tricks on him.

It was time to grow up and accept the obvious. Nancy wasn't coming. She'd made her position perfectly clear, and she intended to stick to it.

He'd been hopeful when the twins sent him that note, telling him that their mommy was miserable. She probably wasn't as bad-off as that, but he had wanted to believe she was at least half as unhappy about this as he was.

Because he was damn near miserable enough to die. His squad partner, fed up with his dark mood, had told him to go out and get himself a woman.

But he didn't want *a* woman, he wanted *the* woman. He wanted Nancy. And the twins. He'd gotten so accustomed to thinking of them as a unit, a family, so accustomed to the idea that he would convince Nancy to marry him, that he stopped thinking of himself as what he was. A single man.

Alone.

Taking a page out of the twins' book, he'd written the ransom note and slipped it under Nancy's door this morning. He'd wanted to give her plenty of time to read it and make up her mind. That way, she'd have more than enough time to get here.

If she was coming.

Which, he thought, glancing at his watch, she obviously wasn't. It was ten after five. Time for him to get up off this bench and go on with his life.

It had been a dumb idea, anyway, sending a ransom note. She probably thought he was an idiot.

Maybe he was, at that.

Guy looked around one last time. She was nowhere in sight. Blowing out a breath, he got up and began to walk to his car.

The bench was empty.

She could see it from here. It was empty. She knew it was the right one, the one he'd told her to come to. But he wasn't on it.

The thought throbbed in her mind, echoing the beat of her high heels as they came down in contact with the pavement as she ran toward the bench. Guy wasn't sitting there, waiting for her.

She'd lost him.

Her lungs felt as if they were going to explode, and the backs of her legs were cramping up. She felt as if she'd been running for miles, instead of just one and a half.

"He's not there, Mommy," Addie cried, heartbroken, running beside Nancy.

A.J. refused to believe it. Guy wouldn't go. He'd wait for them. He *knew* Guy would wait. Like a terrier digging in, he scanned the area, searching for the familiar image.

And then he saw him.

"Mommy, look, over there!" A.J. pointed excitedly. With renewed energy, A.J. sprinted ahead of his mother and sister, after the man who was disappearing around the corner. "Guy! Wait. We're coming! It's us! We're coming!" he yelled at the top of his lungs.

Guy turned. He could have sworn he heard A.J. Yeah, right, just the way he'd seen Nancy walking toward him, he thought deprecatingly.

He was about to leave when he saw first A.J. and then Nancy and Addie in the distance. All three of them were running.

Toward him.

A.J. was almost flying, coming at him as if there were a swarm of bees right behind him.

Getting down on one knee, Guy caught him. It was a little like grabbing a missile in flight. A wonderful missile. The boy threw his arms around him, hugging him tightly. If he heard a sob, Guy pretended not to.

"I knew you'd be here. I just knew it," A.J. said, gasping against his neck.

Addie came next, to claim her hug. Kissing them each one at a time on the head, Guy rose to his feet. And was just in time to catch Nancy as she almost collapsed into his arms.

She was panting as if she were never going to catch her breath. Still, she managed to kiss him, though only fleetingly. Anything more and she'd asphyxiate. Holding on to his arms to steady herself, she gasped for air, unable to talk.

She was here, he thought. Nancy was really here. His eyes caressed her face in disbelief. "I thought you weren't coming."

She shook her head. "Traffic," she breathed out. "So afraid...you'd be...gone." More than afraid. Terrified. Just as terrified as she'd been when she drove to the restaurant that day.

Nancy gulped in air, trying desperately to regulate her breathing enough to tell him why she was late. He held her until she could. And the twins held him, one wrapped around each leg.

It was several more minutes before her chest finally felt as if it wouldn't rupture.

"There was this huge traffic jam. Cars backed up all the way to Main. I was afraid we wouldn't make it in time. That you'd be gone. I left the car in the middle of the street. Probably made it worse," she admitted ruefully. Tears shimmered in her eyes.

"But I was so afraid that if I didn't get here, I'd never see you again."

He held her against him, stroking her hair. God, had anything ever felt so good?

"You wouldn't have," he said honestly. "I decided that if I had to force you into marrying me, then it wouldn't have been right for either of us. I was going to move out."

She raised her head, looking at Guy. She must have been crazy, walking away from him.

"You're not forcing me. And you were right. A little bit of something wonderful *is* so much better than a lifetime of nothing at all." Her eyes told him how much she loved him. And always would. "And I want my little bit of something wonderful. I love you, Guy."

"You don't know how good that sounds to me." He looked at her, his eyes growing serious as his voice softened. "And I love you. Very, very much." Then he laughed, hugging her. The twins took that as a signal to squeeze harder, almost cutting off the circulation to his legs. He didn't mind.

Releasing her, Guy placed a hand on each small shoulder. His very own personal cupids, he thought. He'd always be grateful to them for bringing this about.

"C'mon, kids, let's go get your mother's car and go home. We have a lot of planning to do."

The grins on the twins' faces looked like one long extension of the same expression. And the same thought telegraphed itself through both their minds. They'd done it!

"Think we'll get a ticket?" A.J. asked Guy. Mommy's car was parked almost sideways where they'd gotten out of it and ran for the park.

"I'll take care of it," Guy promised. "That is, if your mother'll marry me."

She tucked one arm around his waist, putting herself between A.J. and Guy. Addie was on Guy's other side, and happy to remain there, from the looks of it. "I think I can live with that."

"You're going to have to," Guy informed her. "Because I'm not letting you go a second time." His gaze took them all in. "Any of you."

"And we," the twins announced in unison, "are never letting you go!"

Nancy turned her mouth up to his. "Ditto," she told him, just before their lips met.

Guy stopped walking and took her into his arms to kiss his future bride properly. His future son cheered.

And this time, Addie didn't poke her brother in the ribs. She joined him.

* * * * *

MILLION DOLLAR SWEEPSTAKES
OFFICIAL RULES
NO PURCHASE NECESSARY TO ENTER

1. To enter, follow the directions published. Method of entry may vary. For eligibility, entries must be received no later than March 31, 1998. No liability is assumed for printing errors, lost, late, non-delivered or misdirected entries.

   To determine winners, the sweepstakes numbers assigned to submitted entries will be compared against a list of randomly, preselected prize winning numbers. In the event all prizes are not claimed via the return of prize winning numbers, random drawings will be held from among all other entries received to award unclaimed prizes.

2. Prize winners will be determined no later than June 30, 1998. Selection of winning numbers and random drawings are under the supervision of D. L. Blair, Inc., an independent judging organization whose decisions are final. Limit: one prize to a family or organization. No substitution will be made for any prize, except as offered. Taxes and duties on all prizes are the sole responsibility of winners. Winners will be notified by mail. Odds of winning are determined by the number of eligible entries distributed and received.

3. Sweepstakes open to residents of the U.S. (except Puerto Rico), Canada and Europe who are 18 years of age or older, except employees and immediate family members of Torstar Corp., D. L. Blair, Inc., their affiliates, subsidiaries, and all other agencies, entities, and persons connected with the use, marketing or conduct of this sweepstakes. All applicable laws and regulations apply. Sweepstakes offer void wherever prohibited by law. Any litigation within the province of Quebec respecting the conduct and awarding of a prize in this sweepstakes must be submitted to the Régie des alcools, des courses et des jeux. In order to win a prize, residents of Canada will be required to correctly answer a time-limited arithmetical skill-testing question to be administered by mail.

4. Winners of major prizes (Grand through Fourth) will be obligated to sign and return an Affidavit of Eligibility and Release of Liability within 30 days of notification. In the event of non-compliance within this time period or if a prize is returned as undeliverable, D. L. Blair, Inc. may at its sole discretion, award that prize to an alternate winner. By acceptance of their prize, winners consent to use of their names, photographs or other likeness for purposes of advertising, trade and promotion on behalf of Torstar Corp., its affiliates and subsidiaries, without further compensation unless prohibited by law. Torstar Corp. and D. L. Blair, Inc., their affiliates and subsidiaries are not responsible for errors in printing of sweepstakes and prize winning numbers. In the event a duplication of a prize winning number occurs, a random drawing will be held from among all entries received with that prize winning number to award that prize.

5. This sweepstakes is presented by Torstar Corp., its subsidiaries and affiliates in conjunction with book, merchandise and/or product offerings. The number of prizes to be awarded and their value are as follows: Grand Prize — $1,000,000 (payable at $33,333.33 a year for 30 years); First Prize — $50,000; Second Prize — $10,000; Third Prize — $5,000; 3 Fourth Prizes — $1,000 each; 10 Fifth Prizes — $250 each; 1,000 Sixth Prizes — $10 each. Values of all prizes are in U.S. currency. Prizes in each level will be presented in different creative executions, including various currencies, vehicles, merchandise and travel. Any presentation of a prize level in a currency other than U.S. currency represents an approximate equivalent to the U.S. currency prize for that level, at that time. Prize winners will have the opportunity of selecting any prize offered for that level; however, the actual non U.S. currency equivalent prize if offered and selected, shall be awarded at the exchange rate existing at 3:00 P.M. New York time on March 31, 1998. A travel prize option, if offered and selected by winner, must be completed within 12 months of selection and is subject to: traveling companion(s) completing and returning of a Release of Liability prior to travel; and hotel and flight accommodations availability. For a current list of all prize options offered within prize levels, send a self-addressed, stamped envelope (WA residents need not affix postage) to: MILLION DOLLAR SWEEPSTAKES Prize Options, P.O. Box 4456, Blair, NE 68009-4456, USA.

6. For a list of prize winners (available after July 31, 1998) send a separate, stamped, self-addressed envelope to: MILLION DOLLAR SWEEPSTAKES Winners, P.O. Box 4459, Blair, NE 68009-4459, USA.

Back by popular demand...

DIANA PALMER's

Long, Tall TEXANS III

They're the best the Lone Star State has to offer—and they're ready for love, even if they don't know it! Available for the first time in one special collection, meet HARDEN, EVAN and DONAVAN.

LONG, TALL TEXANS—the legend continues as three more of your favorite cowboys are reunited in this latest roundup!

Available this July wherever Harlequin and Silhouette books are sold.

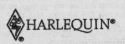

HARLEQUIN®   Silhouette®

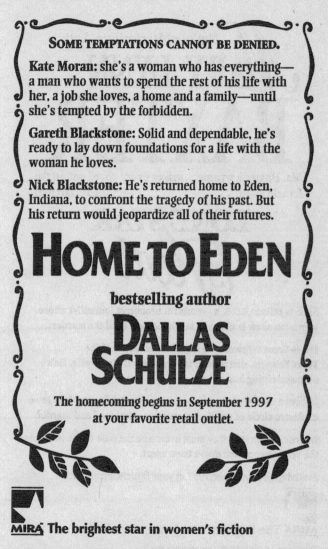